MIDNIGHT FABLES

The dead can't cry.

MRS. RABBIT

BLACKMOOR

ISBN: 978-1-966417-33-0 (Print)

Published in Tennessee by Linda Blackmoor. Linda Blackmoor's titles may be purchased in bulk for educational, business, fundraising, or sales promotional use. For information, please email hello@lindablackmoor.com

First print edition: 2025

Linda Blackmoor
www.LindaBlackmoor.com

TABLE OF CONTENTS

Chapter 1   Page . . . 7

Chapter 2   Page . . . 23

Chapter 3   Page . . . 41

Chapter 4   Page . . . 55

Chapter 5   Page . . . 69

Chapter 6   Page . . . 86

Chapter 7   Page . . . 97

Chapter 8   Page . . . 109

Chapter 9   Page . . . 120

Chapter 10   Page . . . 138

Chapter 11   Page . . . 155

Chapter 12   Page . . . 164

Chapter 13   Page . . . 177

Chapter 14   Page . . . 185

Chapter 15   Page . . . 196

CHAPTER 1

Dawn filtered through the round window of the small cottage grown into the living heart of an ancient oak. Thin, silvery rays traced a pale lattice across the grain of the worn floorboards. The walls themselves were living wood, amber-dark and veined, their knots twisting into whorls that resembled half-moon eyes. The old glass, warped by time, blurred the garden beyond into a watercolor of softened hues and bleeding edges. Weathered curtains, embroidered with tiny bluebells, danced in the morning breeze drifting through the open window. They swayed in mimicry of the dew-kissed chrysanthemums and asters outside, catching and releasing threads of first light.

A pair of flies buzzed against the warped glass with stubborn persistence. *Tap, tap, tapping.* They circled yet never found the narrow gap that might have set them free. The flies had slipped in the night before, when Mr. Rabbit, absorbed in a particularly engrossing chapter on plant medicine, had forgotten to latch the window. Three more lay motionless in the corner of the sill, their eyes still watching, even in death. They were tiny black spots against the sun-bleached wood.

Sunlight collected in warm pools along the floor, the glow dappled by the oak leaves trembling in the breeze overhead. Slowly the light climbed until it brushed Mrs. Rabbit's face where she slept. Her coal-dark fur caught the rays, scattering star-like freckles across her cheeks. She roused, whiskers twitching, then burrowed deeper beneath the patchwork quilt. She had pieced it together many years ago from threadbare scraps of wool. Each square carried its own memory: a length of scarlet cloak inherited from her grandmother, a sliver of green blanket from Mr. Rabbit's formative years, and a matching scrap from a nursery shawl her mother had made in anticipation of Mrs. Rabbit's future kits.

The room still clung to the night's chill, and a draft from the unlatched window fluttered the pages of the botanical compendium resting open on the bedside table. With a resigned sigh, Mrs. Rabbit pushed the quilt aside, releasing a breath of lavender from sachets sewn into the lining. Drawing a thick knitted shawl over her shoulders, she slipped from bed, her feet finding worn slippers by feel. Her breath plumed in the cool air as she padded toward the casement, each step measured so as not to wake her husband.

She rested a paw upon the curved frame of the window and gazed outward at the awakening countryside. A vapor of condensation bloomed on the glass, dissolved, then returned with every exhale. Beyond, the garden stretched before her, shrouded under milk-white mist. The feathery green fronds of carrot tops drooped beneath beads of water, refracting the sunlight in tiny prisms. The rosemary shrub bristled near the fence, its needle-like leaves glittering beside lettuce beds bolting to seed.

Past the low stone wall they had built together, the meadow rolled away in undulating swells of bronze and ochre. Its grasses, tall enough to easily hide a rabbit, swayed in lazy currents. The meadow now sheltered a young family of mice who had recently settled nearby, busily gathering seeds in preparation for the first blanket of snow. At the farthest edge of the meadow, where the land dipped before rising again, the forest loomed. It was black and imposing from this distance, its trunks packed so tightly the trees seemed stitched into a single impenetrable mass.

She lingered at the window for a few more minutes, her gaze sweeping across the landscape, though she wasn't sure what she expected to see. The familiar view, once a source of comfort, now felt charged with a tension she couldn't name. Even the shadows seemed to shift uneasily. In the distance, a single crow gave a low, rasping cry that sliced through the morning air with a sharp note of warning. The family of mice paused, then scurried back toward the safety of their burrow, vanishing underground.

Mrs. Rabbit sighed softly, shaking off the creeping anxiety when she saw nothing else stirring outside. She stepped back from the window and slipped quietly from the bedroom, moving toward the hearth that separated their parlor from the kitchen. The embers from last night's fire lay beneath a cloak of grey ash. Crouching, she stirred them gently, coaxing reluctant flames back to life. The kettle, already filled with water from their well, hung from a soot-black hook on the metal rod above the fire. The water would warm slowly, but there was no hurry.

Mr. Rabbit still slept soundly in the other room, his breathing slow and steady.

Though daylight strengthened, she lit the kerosene lamp hanging near the front door. Its amber glow highlighted the rich reds from the wooden floor and softened the sharp corners of the kitchen. Still sluggish from sleep, she spooned mint and chamomile into the teapot and set two clay mugs onto the dining table Mr. Rabbit had carved by hand. The mug with the hairline crack along its rim found its usual place on his side, just as it had each morning for years.

Above the rafters, the oak's heavy branches groaned, reluctant to greet the dawn. Within the walls, sap flowed in languid rivers, its faint resin perfume mingling with smoke from the hearth. A wandering draft slipped through the doorframe and brushed her ankles with cool fingers. The cottage murmured and settled around her with its familiar sounds.

Still, a thread of unease clung to her like a stubborn cobweb.

From the bedroom, she heard the floorboards creak

beneath shifting weight. Moments later, Mr. Rabbit appeared in the doorway, both paws rubbing sleep from his eyes, ears still flattened and creased from the pillow. His whiskers twitched at the scent of tea drifting through the room.

"Good morning, my four-leaf clover," he murmured, his voice husky yet warm.

She smiled, feeling some of the tension ease from her shoulders. "Good morning."

He crossed to her with unhurried steps, pressed a gentle kiss to her cheek, then crouched beside the hearth to add several small birch logs to the rekindled fire. The wood caught quickly, filling the room with the clean scent of burning bark. His movements held the confidence of long practice. Within their home, there was rarely cause for haste, except when storm clouds gathered; but today's sky stretched pale blue above the morning mist, dotted only by a few soft clouds.

"I'll slice some bread," he said, lifting a grain-crusted loaf from its place near the hearth.

"Please do," she replied. "It'll go lovely with the tea."

They moved around each other in the kitchen with fluid grace. Plates emerged from the cupboard, spoons were placed neatly beside folded cloth napkins, and a small jar of blackberry jam appeared on the table, ready for the bread. Mr. Rabbit hummed a half-remembered tune under his breath as he worked.

The kettle began to whistle. Mrs. Rabbit poured the tea and set it beside the warm loaf. The jam was the last they had of Mr. Fox's sugary preserves, bartered from him at the summer market. He was a peculiar sort, not exactly trustworthy, but he certainly knew how to preserve fruit at the peak of its sweetness.

They settled across from one another at the table and fell into easy conversation, ticking off tasks that remained before autumn gave way to winter: a loose plank on the shed, rosebushes needing pruning, fountains still waiting to be drained.

"Are you still planning to venture into the forest today?" Mrs. Rabbit asked.

She kept her voice light, even as her paw tightened subtly around the handle of her mug.

He nodded. "Mr. Hedgehog needs more mushrooms for his apothecary before the frost sets in. He sent word yesterday that the chanterelles near the eastern hollow might still be good."

She sipped her tea, allowing its warmth to seep slowly into her chest and soothe the restless flutter beneath her ribs. "It's colder than I expected this morning."

Mr. Rabbit smiled, eyes crinkling gently at the corners, though for a fleeting moment his gaze drifted to the kitchen window. "All the more reason to gather what we can. The weather turns quickly this time of year."

Mrs. Rabbit spread jam across a slice of bread, watching as it melted into the crust. She took a small bite, then set the slice back onto her plate.

"You'll stay near the edge? Close to the meadow?" she asked, dusting crumbs from her paws and carefully folding her napkin while awaiting his answer.

Mr. Rabbit chuckled, the sound deep and mellow, like the distant roll of thunder. "Of course. No sense wandering too deep into the forest. Those ferns grow twice my size and in quite a tangled mess. Mr. Hedgehog said he'd be waiting just beyond the treeline."

The hall clock chimed seven, its tone low and faltering, each uneven note lingering in the air. The bronze pendulum swung with labored reluctance, as though burdened by neglect. Mr. Rabbit winced, reminded yet again of the forgotten repairs. He'd intended to mend it weeks ago, but other tasks always took priority.

"Be back before the sun dips below the horizon," she said, careful to keep her voice from sounding like a plea. Yet desperation lingered at the edge of her words, itching at the back of her throat, and she fought the sudden urge to clear it away.

"I promise," he said easily, reaching across the table to brush his paw against hers. His chestnut fur felt slightly coarse, his paws worn smooth from work. "Will you make that delicious carrot and rosemary stew of yours? It always eases the ache in my bones after a long day's foraging."

Mrs. Rabbit smiled and nodded. "Of course. And if you have the time, stop by the orchard for some fresh apples. I'll bake us a nice pie for after supper."

A mischievous glint brightened Mr. Rabbit's eyes. He stood, gently lifted her from her chair, and twirled her once before setting her down again, his grin wide and playful. "My clover, nothing could keep me from your cooking!"

Mrs. Rabbit laughed—a real laugh, bright and full, bubbling up from deep within her. "Go on, then. The sooner you leave, the sooner you'll return." The familiar scent of wild thyme and cedar clinging to him quieted the racing thoughts she'd been trying to ignore all morning.

He finished his bread in a few quick bites, wiped his paws on the cloth, and returned to the bedroom to change. Afterward, he gathered his things from the peg near the door, his satchel slung over one shoulder, the mushroom basket swinging gently from the opposite hand. He opened the satchel once more, paw brushing his flask, trowel, and copper shears. It was an old habit, even though he knew they were exactly where he'd left them.

Before he left, he selected a slim leather notebook, its pages filled with mushroom sketches and neat ink annotations. He tucked a pencil into the spine, pausing as Mrs. Rabbit straightened the green scarf around his neck and smoothed it neatly over the collar of his black coat. The coat's top button was open, revealing his favorite brown overalls and soft linen shirt beneath—both worn thin at the elbows and carefully patched at the knees from seasons of gardening and woodworking. She knew every stitch and patch by heart.

For a brief moment, the room dimmed as the shadow of a hawk swept silently overhead, drifting slowly across the meadow. Then, just as swiftly, it was gone.

"I'll have the stew hot and ready by the time you return," Mrs. Rabbit said, her voice softer now, trembling slightly on the last word. She silently scolded herself for letting the worry show.

"I'm looking forward to it," he said. His hazel eyes held hers, steady and kind, offering comfort without words. He gave her paw a gentle squeeze, the warmth of his touch lingering even after he let go.

She hesitated. Bitterness rose in her throat, sharp and sour, but she swallowed it back down. This morning was no different from a dozen others before it. Mr. Rabbit rarely went off alone, true, but on the few occasions he had, it had never troubled her. Until now.

At the door, he slipped into his rubber boots, then paused. His ears twitched, catching a distant sound, something only he could hear. The moment passed quickly, replaced by a reassuring smile.

She returned it and followed him onto the porch.

Mr. Rabbit stepped down, his boots crunching through dry, curled leaves along the narrow garden path. He lifted the crooked gate to guide it shut; it protested, then settled with a tired thunk as the latch clicked into place.

From somewhere deep within the forest, a shotgun cracked, sharp and sudden.

He froze mid-step. The flicker of alarm on his face was brief, but she caught it before he covered it with another smile.

"That was too far off to fuss over. Probably just a farmer chasing away trouble," he called, lifting a paw in a casual wave as he walked on.

Mrs. Rabbit waved back, though her smile stayed thin.

His figure grew smaller as he crossed the meadow, until only the tips of his ears remained visible. With a final glint of gold thread from his tweed scarf, he vanished into the tall grass.

Mrs. Rabbit lingered on the porch, her sage-green shawl still wrapped around her shoulders, complementing the jade hues of her dress, the lace collar peeking gently above its edge. The mist was rising now, brushed a buttery yellow by the morning sun, yet the light felt strained. The meadow seemed longer than it had this morning; the woods farther away—and yet, somehow, closer too.

She lowered herself into the rocking chair Mr. Rabbit had crafted years ago as a wedding gift, the one with the slightly uneven arm. It creaked beneath her as it often did, though this morning the sound grated against her already fraying nerves.

The stew could wait a little longer, she decided, feeling a gentle tug to watch the meadow's edge a moment more before going back inside. She hoped to catch one last glimpse of him slipping between the trees, but he was already gone.

Her thoughts drifted to the last time they had gone foraging together. They had returned with baskets overflowing with morels, honeycombed caps rich with earth and smoke, and oyster mushrooms, silken clusters delicate as ivory petals. They had feasted that evening, lingering by the fire as rain battered the cottage walls. A few of those mushrooms, dried now, lined the pantry in wax-sealed jars.

A gust stirred a patch of thistles by the steps, drops of water trembling from their purple crowns. Dry sunflower stalks clacked against each other, brittle and hollow. When the wind fell still, a thick silence stretched through the garden.

Then came a sound.

A bark.

Low. Muffled. Carried on the wind.

Her spine went rigid, every vertebra tightening as she strained to listen. Another bark followed, sharper now, closer.

This was not the territorial bark of a farm dog chasing a stoat from the henhouse. These cries held no anger. They were purposeful, cold, and controlled, rising and falling with the discipline of creatures trained for obedience.

Reason urged her to retreat inside. Instead, she stood, rooted to the porch, eyes fixed on the dark seam of trees.

A third bark. Then a fourth. Others joined, weaving into a chorus of pursuit.

The woods at the meadow's edge appeared unchanged, at least visibly. Yet she felt them shift, branches leaning toward the sounds as if they, too, listened with curious intent.

Her eyes searched the shadows between the trees, but found no sign of movement.

And then, through the barking, a new sound.

A piercing cry.

Followed immediately by a sharp crack.

Wood, maybe. Or bone.

The hunt had begun early this year.

CHAPTER 2

Minutes passed. Then an hour. The sun climbed steadily, burning away lingering threads of mist that curled around the garden like skeletal fingers reluctant to release their grip. The final piercing cry, the sickening crack, echoed in Mrs. Rabbit's mind. Her paws, gripping the porch rail, ached from the pressure against splintered wood, leaching warmth from her body. She remained frozen, a furred statue, unaware as time stretched taut. Her gaze never wavered from the shadowed treeline where Mr. Rabbit had disappeared, silently willing his familiar figure to emerge and return home.

Only when the sun beat down on her, its heat becoming unbearable, did she finally emerge from her stupor. She forced herself to accept that Mr. Rabbit would not be returning yet, reassuring herself that if danger had been near, he surely would have come home. She needed to keep busy, and the stew required hours to simmer; with effort, she turned her attention to the herbs and vegetables waiting to be gathered.

Mrs. Rabbit picked up her garden basket by the porch steps and stepped down into their garden. Autumn had already begun gnawing at its edges. A mottled brown crept along the stems of beans and squash, their leaves curled inward, brittle and sere. Her paws sank into the damp soil as she knelt, clumps of earth clinging to her fur. Beneath the disturbed surface, earthworms squirmed, pink and blind, retreating deeper into their tunnels.

The first carrot resisted her efforts, clinging to the soil with stubborn roots. Its leafy top had begun to wilt, limp and yellowing. When it finally yielded, it emerged with a tearing sound. The orange flesh had split lengthwise, exposing hollowed chambers where fat grubs writhed from the unwelcome intrusion of light. She suppressed a shudder, shaking off the larvae and watching them fall one by one, vanishing into dark crevices between clods of mud. She placed the carrot into her wicker basket.

The next carrot emerged teeming with pill bugs. They scattered frantically, segmented carapaces clicking faintly against one another. She brushed dirt from the carrot's flesh with her paw and placed it in the basket. "Only a bit of dirt," she muttered to herself.

The onions made soft, wet plopping sounds as she pulled them from the earth, their papery skins sliding off too easily, exposing layers of bile-colored rot. One split open in her paw, its concentric rings spilling outward, emanating a sickly-sweet stench. Nearby, a forgotten cabbage crouched in the corner of the plot, its bloated, spectral head wrapped in shriveled outer leaves. When she peeled these back, the heart revealed itself threaded with black mold, veins spreading through it like a diseased circulatory system. She placed both the onions and the cabbage alongside the carrots.

She remembered Mr. Rabbit's favorite ingredient, the essential part of her stew. The rosemary shrub drooped under the morning dew, still heavy with silvered droplets where sunlight had yet to reach. She clipped two sprigs. When she crushed the needles of one between her paws and brought them to her nose, the bracing scent was tainted, soured at its edges by the salty tang of early decay. She paused, a frown creasing her brow, then placed the final ingredient into her basket.

A flicker of movement at the edge of her vision made her turn, but she saw only the garden gate swinging slowly on its hinges with a rusty squeal. The latch hung open, though she was certain Mr. Rabbit had secured it behind him—the thunk of it settling into place clear in her memory. She convinced herself perhaps the wind had loosened it, or maybe her memory was playing tricks. Beyond the gate, the meadow remained unchanged, the tall grasses swaying gently in lazy currents.

With the harvest gathered, Mrs. Rabbit returned to the cottage. The door slipped from her grasp, slamming shut behind her with a jarring clap that echoed through the rooms. She jumped, her heart lurching into her throat. Inside, silence pressed heavily against her, transforming the kitchen into something hollow and strange. Even the usual sounds felt distorted: the clock's uneven ticking mocked the irregular rhythm of her own heartbeat. The air itself had thickened, resistant and oppressive, making each breath a conscious effort.

Inside the cottage, the vegetables looked even worse beneath the lantern's light. Colors had darkened into deep purple-black bruises, green mold blooming across wilted leaves like algae in stagnant water. A sweet, cloying smell filled the air, mingling unpleasantly with smoke from the hearth, though her mind was too preoccupied with thoughts of Mr. Rabbit to notice. She tipped her basket onto the wooden counter and reached for a large knife.

Her movements became mechanical, a grim pantomime. Chop. Scrape. Chop. The knife moved without conscious direction, separating what could be salvaged from rot. The blade sank into flesh that yielded like overripe fruit, releasing pockets of gas that stung her eyes and blurred her vision. Beside the chopping board, a pile of refuse grew steadily. Most of the vegetables dissolved into watery pulp, and by the end, what she managed to salvage amounted to less than half of what she'd brought in from the blighted garden. She scraped the vegetables into a heavy iron stew pot, barely noticing as a few remnants of rot slipped in alongside them. Her thoughts drifted elsewhere, drawn toward the shadowed treeline, the echo of the gunshot, and the lingering dread that had haunted her since early morning.

She poured broth from its jar over the vegetables, a thick layer of congealed fat floating on its surface. Placing the pot onto the same hook that had warmed the kettle over the hearth, she watched as the liquid heated slowly, the fatty disc breaking apart and swirling into oily patterns amid the rising bubbles. As she stirred the mixture with a wooden spoon, she noticed a dead grub rise up to its surface. She scooped it out and flicked it into the fire, where it vanished with a sizzling pop.

She placed the lid on the pot with leaden paws. The stew would require hours of simmering to soften what little remained edible. But it would be ready, she assured herself with forced conviction, by the time Mr. Rabbit returned.

If he returned.

The intrusive thought arrived without permission, lodging itself painfully in her throat. She pressed a paw to her chest as though she could physically force it back down, burying it deep within herself where it could no longer torment her.

The kettle, still half-full from their breakfast, had grown cold, but she poured the tea into a fresh cup anyway. She took a small sip, then set the cup down on the table, her expression unreadable, the tea immediately forgotten.

The worn sofa sank deeply beneath her weight as she

settled onto it in the parlor. A faint cloud of dust rose from the cushions, spiraling slowly, lethargically, in the stagnant air. She watched as the motes drifted, dancing like tiny sprites through slanting shafts of sunlight. The walls of the cottage seemed suddenly closer, pressing inward. The corners, usually softened by gentle interplay of light and shadow, were now starkly dark. She felt unseen eyes watching her.

Her gaze drifted to an old silver-framed photograph on the mantelpiece above the hearth. It was a portrait of herself and her younger brother, captured when they were still young kits. They stood posed self-consciously beneath the crooked willow that had dominated the edge of their parents' sprawling garden. Their small, smiling faces stared forward, frozen in time, while the wind, arrested by the camera's click, lifted the willow's trailing branches behind them in graceful, mid-motion arcs. His ears had always bent slightly at the tips—a trait he had disliked fiercely, yet it was inseparably part of him. She had once reassured him, with all the confidence of an older sister, that he would someday grow to love those ears as much as she did.

But as quick and clever as he was, he had still been too

small to outrun the hunting dogs that swept suddenly through their peaceful valley that fateful autumn. Mrs. Rabbit had carried the heavy burden of despair and guilt ever since, remembering how she'd been at the market with their grandmother that day, unable to protect him.

She blinked. For a dizzying instant, her brother's expression in the photograph seemed to shift, flickering briefly with emotion. A part of her mind knew it could only be a trick of the light, a figment conjured by her overwrought imagination, yet she quickly looked away regardless, unable to meet his gaze any longer.

Her ears twitched at every sound—the ticking of the clock, the oak branches scraping softly against one another, a loose shutter knocking once against the outer wall. When it knocked again moments later, she forced herself up and returned outside to latch it. Her paws trembled as she fumbled with the hook, finally managing to secure it into place.

Back inside, she wandered restlessly from room to room, unable to settle the unease building within her. The aged, greenish-brass doorknob of the front door caught her attention, its surface dulled from years of use. Seized by a sudden frantic energy, she found a soft cloth and polished it vigorously until her reflection stared back at her—a warped, elongated caricature. She dusted the bookshelves next, her movements jerky and aimless, before returning to the stew to stir it once more. When she lifted the lid to check its progress, steam rose in greasy coils.

Seeking some semblance of normalcy, some task to anchor her spiraling thoughts, she reached for her sewing basket. Though Mr. Rabbit's drawer already held three freshly darned and neatly folded pairs of woolen socks, she began knitting another pair anyway. The bone needles clicked erratically in her lap. Only a few stitches in, she lost the rhythm, missed a crucial loop, and the entire row unraveled. She released a shaky sigh and tried again. Unable to focus, the needle slipped from her grasp and pricked her paw. A vivid bead of crimson welled up, stark against her dark fur. She lifted the wound instinctively to her mouth, soothing the sting before dropping the yarn and needles back into the sewing basket in defeat.

The afternoon light had begun to fade, surrendering the warmth of day. The sun, retreating toward the western horizon, no longer cast sharp, defined shadows. Instead, they stretched unnaturally long, reaching across the floor in directions that defied the angle of the fading sunlight. The glow had thinned, spreading weakly across the meadow like diluted paint. Grasses that had shone golden and vibrant at midday were now dulled to the lifeless metallic shade of old pewter. She could no longer distinguish individual stalks from the window, only a dense, undulating expanse of grey stretching unbroken toward the waiting line of trees.

The forest seemed closer now, somehow more menacing. Its border, softened in the full daylight, had sharpened into a stark, jagged silhouette.

Mrs. Rabbit lit every lamp in the cottage: one in the parlor, another by the kitchen window, a third in their bedroom. The yellow glow spilled outward, overly harsh for the hour, yet scarcely reached the corners of the rooms. The house grew brighter, but the illumination carried no warmth.

She relit the largest lantern hanging from the hook beside the front door, her paws trembling so badly she nearly dropped the match. She trimmed the wick with painstaking precision until the flame burned high and bright. It wavered and danced, though no draft disturbed the air. Outside, the countryside was swallowed by darkness, leaving only the cottage surrounded by a small circle of lantern-light, like a lighthouse adrift in a sea of night, beckoning Mr. Rabbit home.

Her stomach rumbled, reminding her that she hadn't eaten since breakfast, though she had little appetite. After hours spent simmering over the low fire, the stew was finally ready. Using oven mitts, she lifted the heavy pot carefully and placed it on a trivet in the center of the dining table. She ladled it into a bowl, watching it stretch from pot to spoon in strands. The broth had congealed at the edges, thickened unpleasantly. The taste proved worse than the smell—spoiled and oily, coating her tongue in a greasy film.

She forced herself to swallow a mouthful, but her body immediately rebelled in warning. Determined to quiet her hunger, she tried a second spoonful, only to bite down on something gritty that popped between her teeth. She spat discreetly into her napkin, unwilling to look at what it had been.

The bowl joined her cold cup of tea, both now abandoned.

She opened the front door again, her breath misting in the rapidly cooling air. It was the third time she had done so in the past hour, and each time, more of the remaining light had drained away, leaving the world increasingly desolate. Even the moon and stars had hidden themselves behind clouds she could not see. The narrow footpath beyond the garden gate had disappeared entirely into the gloom. The meadow had become a featureless dark ocean, the forest at its edge looming like a gaping, hungry mouth.

"Mr. Rabbit?" she called, her voice wavering.

Silence answered her. Then, slowly at first, the cicadas began their nightly symphony. Their raspy, chittering song rose gradually, swelling to a deafening crescendo before fading away once more. She stood there for a long moment, struggling to conjure comforting images: Mr. Rabbit seated comfortably in Mr. Squirrel's cozy treetop home, perhaps sharing a mug of warm cider, blissfully unaware of the retreating sun in a drunken stupor; or maybe still chatting with old Mr. Hedgehog, sharing a companionable pipe, surprised by how quickly the day had passed and deciding to stay the night for safety's sake. But these fragile excuses unraveled almost as swiftly as she created them.

Mr. Rabbit was meticulous, thoughtful—he would never break a promise so carelessly. He would never willingly leave her waiting, consumed by worry, without sending word.

She built up the fire, stacking logs until it roared—higher and hotter than necessary—but she was desperate to dispel the visceral tremor that had settled like ice into her bones, leaving her shivering. Flames licked and crackled, greedily consuming the driest logs with fierce hunger. She sank into the armchair nearest the hearth, the one with worn armrests, and wrapped herself tightly in a crocheted blanket the color of robin eggs.

Moths, drawn by the unfamiliar brightness, began battering themselves against the windowpanes, their delicate, powdery wings leaving pale dust on the glass. They were relentless in their attempts to reach the lantern's glow, heedless of the unyielding barrier, blissfully ignorant of the certain death awaiting them should they ever touch the flame.

She resolved inwardly that she would remain awake. She would listen for the creak of the garden gate's hinges, the crunch of familiar footsteps on the path, the scrape of muddy boots against the porch.

Yet sleep overtook her in restless fits.

Once she woke with a jolt, her chin pressed uncomfortably against her chest, certain she'd heard the distinct sound of the door handle turning. Another time, she startled bolt upright at what unmistakably sounded like the creak of floorboards in the bedroom. Each time, her heart leaped with hope—but as her eyes adjusted to the dim, firelit room, the cottage remained achingly empty. The fire had burned low while she slept, dwindling to a sullen mound of glowing coals. No boots stood by the door; no familiar coat hung from its peg.

The night deepened. The windows, once welcoming portals to the outside world, became black mirrors, reflecting only her own hunched, desolate form in the flickering lanternlight.

Then, sometime in that empty expanse between midnight and the first hint of dawn, she heard barking.

For a moment, she thought she had dreamed it, a phantom echo conjured by her fears. But then it came again, faint yet unmistakable. Farther away than the morning before, yet clearly recognizable: the familiar bark of hunters' dogs.

The sound faded as quickly as it had come, carried off by the mournful sigh of the wind.

At last, a grudging light returned to the world, though it was not a clear, bright dawn. Instead, morning arrived cloaked in a fog so dense, so impenetrable, that it smothered the landscape like a heavy white cloth. Just as darkness had obscured the world the night before, now it remained hidden, dissolved into a colorless, featureless smear.

She rose slowly from the armchair, her joints stiff and protesting from the long night. Her entire body ached with a pervasive, lingering soreness.

Mr. Rabbit had not come home.

She moved to the window, startled by the cold radiating sharply from the glass.

"I'm coming to find you," she whispered to the blank wall

of white that concealed whatever lay beyond. Her voice sounded raw, strained from disuse and unshed tears. Yet speaking the words aloud solidified her determination.

She dressed quickly, her movements deliberate, imbued now with grim purpose. She gathered her own worn satchel—the one usually resting beside Mr. Rabbit's—and filled it with a small loaf of day-old bread, a wedge of hard cheese, and a flask of fresh water. From the small locked cabinet beside the sofa, she retrieved her largest bone sewing needle. Intended for heavy upholstery, its point had been sharpened years ago into perfect fineness. Its smooth weight in her paw felt unexpectedly reassuring. Carefully, she slipped it into the deep pocket of her dress.

Her coat was buttoned tightly at her neck. Her sturdiest walking boots, usually reserved for harsh winter weather, were securely laced to the ankles. She gripped a lantern, its oil freshly replenished and glowing with a steady light, and stepped firmly onto the porch.

The garden, shrouded in dense fog, appeared alien in its transformation. Every gossamer spiderweb strung between the porch railings shimmered with crystal droplets. The air carried an unpleasant scent of mildew.

Mrs. Rabbit caught another flicker of movement at the periphery of her vision and turned sharply, senses on high alert, though the fog clouded her sight. But no one was there. Only the old, rusted weathervane atop the dilapidated shed beside the house moved within the dense fog, its arrow-shaped tail slowly turning.

Her own garden had become a place of ghosts.

She walked determinedly, the hem of her dress brushing against the damp grass, growing heavier as it absorbed moisture. Her breathing seemed unnaturally loud in the oppressive silence. No birds sung their morning greeting; no insects buzzed or chirped.

She pushed through the tall meadow grasses, hoping she was heading in the right direction, and felt a surge of relief when the edge of the trees finally appeared before her.

The birches stood in neat ranks, their slender trunks like silent, watchful soldiers guarding the woods from the outside world—or perhaps guarding the world from whatever lay hidden within the forest's depths.

She drew a deep, steadying breath, the fog-laden air heavy in her lungs. Then, with courage she did not truly feel, but willed herself to summon, she stepped into the forest.

CHAPTER 3

Fog clung to the first ranks of trees like unspun wool, muffling the world into a silence that felt almost sacred. Mrs. Rabbit paused just inside the woodline, lantern lifted, its glow catching on beads of moisture that hung suspended in the air. The forest seemed to hold its breath around her, waiting.

The air smelled of cold earth and wet bark, a darker, deeper scent than the meadow behind her. Decay lingered beneath, the sweet-sour musk of leaves returning to soil, fungal threads weaving through fallen limbs. She drew in a shallow breath, steadying herself.

The birch trunks were banded with lichens the color of winter sage. Some grew in strange shapes, like sigils meant to warn away unwelcome intruders. Others spread in loose, irregular patches that seemed to shift in the lantern light. Between the trees, ferns unfurled their fronds, some reaching as high as her shoulders, their undersides dotted with spores that would soon scatter on the wind.

She wrapped her coat tighter, nerves tugging in her belly. Every crackle of fallen leaves beneath her feet seemed too loud, announcing her presence to the silent woods. The forest floor was carpeted thick with seasons of decomposition, creating a springy surface that gave slightly with each step.

Her eyes adjusted gradually to the gloom. A large antler jutted from the ground ahead, half-buried in moss, bleached pale and sharp. The moss itself grew in strange patterns here, forming perfect circles in some places, as if marking spots where something had died and enriched the soil. Something rustled in the undergrowth, she kept her gaze fixed ahead, refusing to investigate.

The path Mr. Rabbit would have taken wound between moss-cushioned roots that resembled arthritic fingers clawing up from below. Some of these roots belonged to oaks so old their trunks had split and hollowed, creating dark caverns where anything might shelter. Shelf fungi sprouted from the dying wood in overlapping plates, their surfaces painted in bands of rust and cream. A large trunk had fallen over a clear stream that bubbled as it made its way over rocks.

She stepped onto the trunk to cross over, noting how the stones had been worn smooth by countless years of flowing water, but her boot slipped on the slick surface. She steadied herself, balancing with her arms outstretched. Broken bark splashed into the water, tiny beetles scurried away from underfoot. She slowly made her way across then jumped down and continued forward.

The trees began to thin, giving way to an unexpected clearing. At first, she thought it might be a natural meadow, but as her lantern swept across the open ground, the light caught on weathered stone. Not the rounded shapes of boulders, but rectangular forms. Rows of them, leaning at odd angles.

Gravestones.

A forgotten cemetery now claimed by the woods. Most of the markers had fallen or crumbled, their inscriptions worn to illegible marks by centuries of rain. Ivy crept across some, and lichen bloomed in the carved letters of others, filling the voids with living script. Wild roses had taken root among the graves, their blooms long faded, leaving behind clusters of orange hips that glowed like tiny lanterns in the dim light.

Human names, human dates, all belonging to those who had lived and died long before Mrs. Rabbit was born. Some stones bore symbols she didn't recognize: crossed keys, anchors, hands pointing skyward. The oldest markers were simple slabs, while newer ones, though still ancient by her reckoning, showed more elaborate carving.

At the center stood a stone angel, its face eroded to a featureless oval, wings half-crumbled, arms outstretched in an eternal gesture of either welcome or warning. A dusting of frost rimmed its shoulders despite the season, glittering in the lantern light. Around its base, someone had once planted bulbs that still pushed through each spring, though their blooms had grown wild and strange over the years.

Mrs. Rabbit hesitated at the edge of the cemetery. There were stories about such places, old places where the barrier between living and dead grew thin. Mr. Mole claimed his grandfather once saw figures moving between these stones on moonless nights, their footsteps making no sound as they passed. The old badger who lived near the village swore he'd heard singing from this very cemetery on some winter nights, though no living soul was present.

"Nonsense," she whispered to herself, forcing her way forward. She didn't believe in tales meant to frighten young ones. The path cut directly through the graveyard; there was no way around. As she walked between the stones, her lantern cast long shadows that seemed to follow her movements with unnatural persistence. The ground felt different here, softer, almost yielding beneath her weight, as though reluctant to support the living. Patches of moss grew thicker between the graves, muffling her footsteps to near silence.

The fog began to thin as the morning rose, revealing flashes of color beneath the canopy, rusted copper leaves still clinging to beeches, scarlet berries freckling dogwood branches. Yet even this beauty felt fragile, as if autumn's touch might shatter it.

She called out his name once more, hopeful.

"Mr. Rabbit?"

The sound dissolved before it reached the higher limbs, absorbed by the watchful silence. Only a crow responded, its harsh caw breaking from somewhere unseen, ending in what sounded almost like laughter.

Not far ahead, the path widened into a hollow where the ground bowed inward like a shallow bowl. Years of runoff had carved channels in the earth, creating a natural drainage system that kept the depression from flooding. A sagging burlap tarp, patched and re-patched with mismatched scraps, had been strung between two birches to keep the worst of the rain from a scatter of crates and barrels. There, sorting cork-stoppered jars into organized rows, was Mr. Hedgehog.

He was smaller than she remembered, quills sharp but thinning in patches that revealed pink skin beneath. His muzzle had gone snowy with age, and one eye clouded with cataracts, giving him a perpetually startled expression. A cedar-wood cane, its handle worn to a glossy sheen from years of use, leaned against a stump close by. His workshop showed the accumulated oddities of decades, bundles of herbs hung from every available surface, their scents mingling into something both medicinal and mysterious.

When she stepped into the clearing, her lantern light swept across his workstation. Shelves made of scavenged planks sagged under the weight of hundreds of glass containers, some no bigger than thimbles, others as large as water jugs. Their contents glowed eerily in the light: slivers of dried chanterelles, curls of tarragon, tiny brown nuts for winter tonics. But there were stranger items too, things Mrs. Rabbit couldn't immediately identify.

One shelf held jars of cloudy liquid in which pale objects floated, some resembled fingers, others coiled like sleeping snakes. Another contained glass vials of powder in colors nature rarely produced: electric blue, sulfurous yellow, a red so dark it appeared black until the light struck it just so. A collection of teeth, too large for any woodland creature, had been arranged in a spiral pattern on a flat stone, their roots stained with soil. Beside them, a mortar and pestle sat waiting, its bowl stained with residue that had dried to a dark crust.

"Good morning, Mr. Hedgehog," she called, pitching her voice gently so as not to startle his failing ears.

The old fellow straightened, joints cracking audibly like twigs underfoot. His small eyes brightened with recognition beneath bristling brows. "Well, if it isn't Mrs. Rabbit," he said, accent thick and warm. "Out early, and in this damp! You'll ruin that fine coat."

"A little moisture won't hurt it," she managed, though her smile wavered. Her gaze kept drifting to the jars behind him, where what looked like an eye blinked slowly in murky liquid. "I'm looking for my husband. He left yesterday and hasn't come home."

Mr. Hedgehog's quills flattened slightly, concern flickering across his features. He set a jar aside, its contents emitting a faint glow even after he'd released it, and beckoned her nearer. "Come, rest a moment. You're trembling."

Carefully she knelt on a dry patch of moss beside him, lantern set between them like a small campfire. The light caught the underside of his quills and made him appear older than his years. Around them, the tools of his trade lay scattered: tiny glass droppers, silver measuring spoons tarnished with age, bundles of string for tying herbs.

"You saw him yesterday?" she asked, glancing at a bundle of dried herbs hanging from the tarp.

"Aye." He lowered himself onto a stump, cane across his knees. A small bone, perhaps from a bird, had been tied to the handle with red thread. "He met me just after dawn. Helped me hunt the last of the autumn caps. Fine specimens, too—your husband has a nose for fungus better than any badger's."

"Was everything well?"

"As well as weather allows. We filled two baskets by midday." He tilted his head, thoughtful. Behind him, a row of small clay pots rattled faintly, though nothing had touched them. "He spoke of fetching apples from Mr. Squirrel's orchard after we parted. Said you'd planned a pie."

She nodded. "Yes. He promised to be back before sundown."

The hedgehog's gaze softened, his cloudy eye catching the lantern light in a way that made it appear to glow from within. "Then something must have delayed him, that's all. Those orchards sit close to the valley creek. Water rises this time of year; perhaps he took the long way."

She wanted to believe it, but the image of hunters' dogs, their low baying, shivered through her memory. "Did you notice anything unusual yesterday? Any sign of hunters or their dogs?"

Mr. Hedgehog's brow furrowed. "No dogs. Only a family of deer, enjoying the wild elderberries that are finally in season." He tapped his cane against the stump, and the bone tied to it swung gently. "Though we did hear a shot, distant, while we worked. Sent the jays shrieking."

A small sound of despair escaped her. He laid a consoling paw over hers. "Fear breeds its own phantoms, Mrs. Rabbit. Your husband is quick-footed and clever. Give him the chance to find his way."

"Thank you. I can't seem to sit idle. I'll head to the orchard, see if Mr. Squirrel met him."

The old hedgehog pushed himself up with effort. "When you find your husband, send him 'round. I've a jar of honeyed truffles set aside for the two of you."

She promised she would, though the thought of eating anything prepared from those strange jars made her stomach tighten. She lifted the lantern and backed away, watching as he tottered toward his jars of medicine and oddities, mumbling to himself. She drew a deep breath and turned to face the path eastward.

As the forest thinned toward the valley, sunlight seeped beneath the branches, pooling in golden patches across the leaf-strewn ground. Trees that had seemed welcoming in past visits now twisted away from the path, their branches forming cage-like patterns overhead. Old blazes marked some of the trunks—cuts made by human hands to mark the trail, now healed over but still visible as pale scars in the bark.

The orchard lay beyond a low ridge, and she smelled it before she saw it: the crisp sweetness of wind-fallen apples mingled with the damp spice of rotting leaves.

The ridge itself was steep, the path cutting back and forth to ease the climb. Someone had placed stones at the turns, creating rough steps that had settled unevenly over the years. Wild grapevines tangled through the underbrush, their leaves already turning crimson and gold. A few withered clusters of grapes still clung to the vines, too sour for eating but perfect for the birds that would soon descend to feast.

Crows hopped between crooked trunks, picking at bruised fruit, wings flashing blue-black in the filtered light. They paused as she approached, black eyes following her movement with an intelligence that felt almost predatory. One let out a low, gurgling croak that seemed to echo longer than it should. Others took up the call, creating an eerie symphony that made her quicken her pace.

She slipped through a small gate, its latch bound with twine, and paused beside a barrel overflowing with russet apples. A sign in Mr. Squirrel's tidy handwriting read:

HELP YOURSELF, TRADE LATER.

It swung gently, though there was no breeze, the metal chain holding it creaking with a slow, tired groan. The barrel itself showed years of use, its wood stained dark from countless seasons of apple juice seeping through the slats.

"Mr. Squirrel?" she called, stepping between the rows. No answer came. Only the slow drip from leaf tips and the soft slap of rotten fruit falling from high limbs.

The orchard had always felt cheerful on market days, chattering with neighbors trading recipes and gossip. Today, though, it felt different. The trees seemed to cower, their trunks hunched and twisted. The grass beneath her boots squelched, releasing small puffs of cold air that rose into the sunlight and disappeared. Somewhere in the distance, a woodpecker hammered rapidly on a tree, the sound sharp and insistent. Between the rows, old ladders leaned against trunks, forgotten after the last harvest, their rungs patchy green.

At the midpoint of the orchard, the terrain dipped into a low hollow carpeted with bruised apples. Here the trees were older, their bark furrowed like solemn faces watching her pass. Dark hollows in their trunks resembled eyes and mouths frozen in expressions of dismay. Some bore the scars of old pruning, branches cut away years ago leaving knots that had healed into grotesque shapes. A limb as thick as her arm had cracked and fallen across the path, its splintered end sharp as a spear. She climbed over it, her dress snagging on rough bark. On the other side she stumbled, lantern swinging wildly, and something green caught the light.

She froze. Ten paces ahead, half-buried beneath a scatter of leaves, lay a strip of cloth no wider than her paw. The mossy ground around it was disturbed, muddy impressions marking the surface like the aftermath of a struggle. Carefully, she knelt.

The fabric was dark green tweed, softened by wear and threaded with tiny flecks of gold, exactly the wool she had chosen last winter, when the cold grew bitter and Mr. Rabbit complained his old scarf had worn thin. She lifted it with trembling paws. One edge was frayed, as if it had been torn rather than cut. Along that edge, a rusty stain had dried, mottling the weave.

The metallic smell rose from the fabric, confirming what her eyes already knew. Her fingers traced the torn edge, feeling where the threads had been pulled apart by force. The stain had set deep into the fibers, darkening them to nearly black at the center. She pressed the scrap to her chest, a sob catching in her throat.

Blood.

CHAPTER 4

The rusty stain on the tweed formed an unsettling pattern, spreading through the fibers like a dark bloom. She turned the fragment over, her brow furrowed, her fingers tracing the ragged edges where the fabric had been violently torn. Whatever had ripped this from her husband had done so with terrible force. The threads were stretched and broken, some hanging loose. A wave of nausea washed over her, and she instinctively pressed a paw against her churning stomach.

A twig snapped behind her.

She whirled, the lantern lifting in a reflexive arc, her heart leaping into her throat. The flame swung wildly in its glass cage, casting twisted shadows across the gnarled limbs of the apple trees. For a moment, the shadows seemed to reach for her with crooked fingers.

Mr. Squirrel stood frozen mid-step, his normally sleek tail now sodden and drooping with dew, tangled with stray twigs and clinging burrs. His once-jaunty blue vest, the vibrant hue of summer cornflowers, hung crooked across his narrow shoulders, its small brass buttons tarnished to a dull, verdigris green. Water dripped steadily from his whiskers, creating tiny puddles at his feet.

"Mercy, Mrs. Rabbit, I'm so sorry," he whispered, his voice thin and reedy with alarm. "Didn't mean to startle you."

The lantern light flickered across his face, revealing new lines of worry etched deep into the fur around his twitching whiskers. His small paws trembled as he wrung them together, a nervous habit she'd never seen him display before. He dug his claws into the muddy earth, leaving small furrows in the soft ground.

Mrs. Rabbit drew a shaky breath, forcing air into her constricted lungs. The cold morning air burned as she inhaled. "It's all right," she managed, though her voice trembled slightly. She held up the bloodied scrap of tweed, watching as recognition dawned in his eyes. "But tell me, Mr. Squirrel, have you seen my husband?

I found this."

Mr. Squirrel's gaze landed on the stained fabric, his small, dark eyes widening with evident distress. The color seemed to drain from beneath his fur. "Oh dear," he murmured. With a shaky paw, he brushed damp fur back from his forehead, droplets clinging stubbornly around his anxious eyes. "Yes, I saw him yesterday. Mid-afternoon, perhaps. He was passing through the orchard, his mushroom basket swinging at his side, humming a tune."

"Did he speak with you? Did he say where he was headed next?" The questions tumbled out faster than she intended, desperation creeping into her voice.

"He didn't get a chance to say much beyond a quick hello and a friendly wave," Mr. Squirrel replied, his tail twitching with increasing agitation. His breath hitched and puffed white in the cool air. The morning had grown colder while they stood there, autumn asserting itself with each passing moment.

He hesitated, his gaze flicking nervously towards the shadowy edge of the forest where the apple trees gave way to darker woods. The boundary seemed more ominous now, a threshold between the familiar and the unknown. "He never made it past the first row of trees. Mr. Fox flagged him down by the old fence." The squirrel's eyes darted towards the dense treeline, where the foliage was thick. "They spoke for a little while, their words too soft for me to hear from where I was gathering fruit. I was up in the branches, you see, checking which apples might still be salvageable. Then... then Mr. Rabbit followed Mr. Fox in the direction of his den."

A cold knot of dread tightened in Mrs. Rabbit's chest, sending icy tendrils through her veins. The world seemed to tilt slightly, as if the ground beneath her feet had become unreliable. Mr. Fox's den wasn't the kind of place Mr. Rabbit ever visited. While they occasionally exchanged goods at the market, maintaining the polite fiction of neighborly commerce, a deep-seated distrust lingered between them. Mr. Fox had a disconcerting habit of flashing his sharp canines before slowly licking them, his tongue deliberately tracing each pointed tip, followed by a sly grin. There was always a hint of hunger in his narrow, calculating gaze, as if he were perpetually measuring the distance between himself and his next meal.

"And you're certain?" she pressed, the words emerging strained with disbelief. "They left together?"

"I am," he said, his voice barely above a whisper. He shifted his weight from foot to foot, creating new impressions in the mud. "Mr. Fox was carrying a sack that looked heavy, bulging like it was filled with stones. He kept shifting it from one shoulder to the other, as if the weight troubled him."

Mr. Squirrel glanced again at the blood-stained tweed in her paw. His eyes widened further, pupils dilating with fear, and he took a half-step back without seeming to notice. The movement disturbed a cluster of fallen leaves, sending them skittering across the wet ground. "They disappeared together beyond the ridge, heading toward Mr. Fox's home. I didn't think much of it at the time. Sometimes folk have private business, after all. But not long after, a gunshot echoed through the trees. I got spooked and went straight home, barricading my door. The hunters... they're early this year."

His frightened gaze darted back to the treeline, his tail now a blur of anxious movement, a stark contrast to his forced attempt at composure.

"Their dogs are getting faster, Mrs. Rabbit."

Mrs. Rabbit's mind reeled, trying to make sense of the disjointed pieces of the morning: the gunshot, the baying of hounds, and Mr. Rabbit following Mr. Fox towards his isolated den. The pieces refused to form a coherent picture. Mrs. Rabbit couldn't imagine any reason Mr. Rabbit would choose to detour back into the woods with Mr. Fox, especially not when he'd promised to be home before dark. And now this... the bloodied cloth.

She folded the scrap of tweed with painstaking care, as if rough handling it might destroy the only clue she had. The fabric seemed to resist being tucked away, clinging to her fingers before she managed to slip it into the pocket of her coat. "Thank you, Mr. Squirrel," she murmured, her voice flat and distant to her own ears.

"Please," she urged gently, steeling her resolve as much for Mr. Squirrel's sake as her own, "tell Mr. Hedgehog what has happened. Let him know I've gone to find my husband. If darkness falls before I return, let everyone know to be vigilant. Lock their doors, shutter their windows. My husband may simply be delayed, but danger could be very close."

Mr. Squirrel nodded fervently, a visible shiver rippling through his small frame from nose to tail. "I'll warn the entire hollow immediately, Mrs. Rabbit. Word travels swiftly around here, especially with the change in season bringing everyone together for the harvest preparations. Please be careful. The ridge path is treacherous even in good weather. Keep to the right; the left side drops sharply into the old bog. It's claimed unwary travelers before, sucked them down into the dark water until nothing remains but a few lingering bubbles on the surface."

"Thank you, Mr. Squirrel. I will heed your advice." She extended her paw and briefly grasped his, squeezing it gently. They stood there for a moment, silent in their shared anxiety, while around them the orchard seemed to hold its breath.

She slipped the lantern's handle over her wrist and turned resolutely towards the tangled woods. Behind her, the orchard fell silent once more, broken only by the wet splat of overripe apples falling from the rain-soaked branches.

The path began beneath a crooked alder, its mossy trunk glowing with an eerie phosphorescence in the dim forest light. The tree's trunk split near its base, forming an arching gateway that seemed to beckon her deeper into the wilderness. Its bark was scarred with raking claw marks, some old and healed over, others fresh enough that sap still wept from the wounds. The marks trailed upwards until they vanished into the dense foliage overhead, as if something had climbed in desperate haste.

Mrs. Rabbit moved with a determined swiftness, trusting the lantern's bright beam to push back against the darkness. The glass chimney had begun to fog with condensation, blurring the flame within. She paused to wipe it clear with the edge of her coat, the brief darkness making her acutely aware of how alone she was. The lantern swung rhythmically from her wrist once she resumed walking, its gentle sway almost hypnotic.

A wind hissed through the high branches, shaking loose the sharp resinous scent of pine pitch. Droplets of sap fell like amber tears, some still warm from the tree's heart. She strained her ears, listening intently for the telltale baying of hounds, the crack of a hunter's rifle, any sound that might explain the blood on Mr. Rabbit's scarf. But she heard only the soft crunch of her own boots on the grit of the path and the occasional skittering of unseen creatures retreating from the beam of her light. Once, she caught a glimpse of multiple eyes reflecting yellow in the darkness before they vanished.

Halfway up the gradual slope, she discovered a clear scuff mark in the mud: the distinct print of Mr. Rabbit's sturdy boot, its outline crisp in the soft earth. The sight of it made her heart leap with both hope and fear. She knelt beside it, her paw hovering just above the impression, afraid that touching it might somehow erase this proof of his passage. She recognized the pattern of his sole, the slight uneven wear along the outer edge where he favored his right side after an old injury, the small nick in the heel from when he'd stepped on a piece of broken glass last spring. The edges of the print were still sharp, preserved by the morning cold. A second, lighter but deliberate track overlapped his: narrow and pointed. The two sets of tracks walked side-by-side for a short distance before veering sharply towards a break in the dense brambles. Nearby, a shelf of sandstone jutted out from the hillside, its surface dark with moisture.

She followed the deviation, hope and dread braided so tightly in her chest she could no longer tell them apart. Each breath came shallow and quick. The path narrowed abruptly. The ferns grew thicker here, some reaching above her head, their fronds unfurling like skeletal hands.

At the sandstone ledge lay Mr. Rabbit's mushroom basket.

It rested upright on the stone, its woven handle intact but listing to one side. The careful weaving she recognized as his handiwork, each willow strand placed with patience and skill. But its contents were gone, save for a single, cracked chanterelle that had rolled into a corner, its delicate gills bruised and darkening to an unhealthy brown. She lifted the basket, turning it in the lantern light. Small tears marred one side, as if claws had raked across it. She traced her paw over the splintered weave, feeling the rough edges. The basket carried a faint odor of fox musk, sharp and unmistakable, and beneath that, the lingering earthy scent of the fungi it once held. A few pine needles clung to the bottom and a single red fox hair, caught in the weaving.

The ridge ahead was a steep climb, marked by a narrow footpath where fallen leaves had been recently kicked aside, revealing the dark soil beneath. She pressed onward, her legs burning with the effort, her chest cinched tight

with more than exertion. Each step took her farther from
the relative safety of home, deeper into territory where her
kind rarely ventured.

The light thinned despite the early hour, the sun had
begun its retreat behind a gathering bank of ominous
clouds. Through fleeting breaks in the dense canopy, she
caught glimpses of a washed-out sky being devoured by
darkness. Thick, storm clouds were rolling in from the
west, their undersides bruised purple and gray. It was
reassurance that night hadn't yet fallen, though the
approaching storm seemed eager to bring its own kind of
darkness. A fine rain began to fall, slicking her coat and
boots. The lantern sputtered once, its flame momentarily
wavering in a dance of orange and blue, then steadied, the
glass protecting it from the increasing dampness.

Now and then, a gust of wind slid between the trees,
carrying fragmented scents that told their own stories: the
lingering acridity of gunpowder hanging in the air like a
phantom, the faint, mineral smell of a hidden creek
somewhere out of sight, and something else that made her
nose wrinkle. Death. Old death, the kind that had
returned to earth but left its memory in the soil. Each gust
teased the fur along her ears. She kept her gaze fixed on

the small, wavering corridor of light ahead, unwilling to look too deeply into the woods on either side, where indistinct shapes seemed to shift and move just at the periphery of her vision.

The ground revealed a tangle of thin, exposed roots that writhed like veins. Soon, the path leveled out onto a broad shelf of granite that jutted precariously from the steep hillside. The stone was slick with rain, treacherous underfoot. A thick mist coiled in its shallow hollows, opaque and ghost-pale, moving with a slow, deliberate purpose that seemed independent of the wind.

Mrs. Rabbit paused at the rim of the granite shelf, her lantern lifted high, waiting for the clinging fog to dissipate. The mist seemed almost alive, reaching out with vaporous tendrils that dissolved at the touch of her light. When it did not retreat, she pressed forward anyway, letting intuition guide her where her sight failed. She knew the narrow track curved gently to the right and would begin its final, steep ascent towards the ridge's crown; Mr. Fox's den waited somewhere beyond that rise, burrowed within the stone that formed the hill's backbone.

Inside the swirling fog, sound warped and altered. Her own footsteps seemed to echo from the wrong directions, as if invisible companions walked beside her. She kept her pace slow and measured, testing the ground before committing her weight.

A low roll of thunder rumbled across the distance, a sound felt more than heard, a deep vibration that passed through the ground and into the marrow of her bones. The stone beneath her feet seemed to tremble in response. She glanced upwards: the dense canopy quivered as if in answer, releasing a fresh shower of raindrops that fell with increased urgency. The drops were larger now, heavier, each one a small cold shock against her fur. The breeze that followed carried the unmistakable scent of the quickly approaching storm, the clean tang of ozone.

Beyond the skeletal trees, strands of ivy began to appear, weak, tentative tendrils at first that crept along the ground and wound around the bases of smaller saplings. Then came thicker ropes that crawled across moss-covered boulders in dark, sinuous knots. The ivy grew denser as she climbed, some vines as thick as her wrist, their leaves dark and glossy with rain. She had heard rumors that these relentless vines led directly to Mr. Fox's den high on the ridge, marking his territory as surely as any scent marker.

A surge of relief, sharp and sudden, swelled within her. She was agonizingly close to finding answers, close to discovering what had befallen her husband. But the relief was immediately tempered by a fresh wave of dread that anchored her to the spot. She didn't know what waited beyond the stone, what the sight of that bloody scrap truly meant, and why Mr. Rabbit would ever willingly go to Mr. Fox's home.

She gripped the lantern handle tighter, the metal now slick with rain and her own nervous sweat. Drawing in a deep breath of the storm-charged air, she straightened her spine with a newfound resolve. Her jaw clenched as she approached Mr. Fox's lair, each step a small act of courage against the fear that threatened to turn her back.

And somewhere, hidden amongst the rain-silvered trees, a pair of slitted copper eyes watched her approach.

CHAPTER 5

Mrs. Rabbit turned slowly.

The sensation began at the base of her spine, a cold awareness that slithered upward, like frost creeping across a windowpane. Her fur bristled, each dark strand lifting as if swept by a current of invisible electricity. Whatever watched her remained hidden among the rain-darkened trees, but its gaze pressed against her like a physical weight. Her heart stammered against her ribs with such force she feared it might crack them, its rhythm wild and uneven. Yet her paws remained fixed to the forest floor, as if the roots below had wound themselves around her ankles, binding her in place.

In the narrow space between heartbeats, a figure materialized from the dense shadows. It appeared first as a broken silhouette against the darker woods beyond, ragged edges of autumn-red fur caught in shafts of dying light that filtered through the storm clouds. A thin muzzle emerged next, unnaturally elongated, followed by ears laid flat against a narrow skull. The eyes blinked open slowly, twin embers that floated without a face, copper pools that caught what little light remained and returned it changed.

He stepped forward, emerging fully into a patch of fractured sunlight that had managed to pierce the canopy. The brightness fell across him in harsh, unforgiving bands, revealing a form so altered by injury that for a moment, Mrs. Rabbit doubted her own eyes. This creature bore little resemblance to the sleek predator she knew. Mr. Fox's once-lustrous coat hung in tattered clumps, scraped away in places to reveal raw flesh beneath that glistened with seepage. Dark streaks of dried blood matted his fur where wounds had wept, only to reopen and weep again with each labored movement. From his limbs protruded vicious thorns like cruel needles driven deep, their barbed tips disappearing into swollen flesh.

"Mr. Fox?" The question barely escaped her throat, caught between disbelief and horror.

No answer came. His weight seemed to list dangerously with each movement, as if he might topple at any moment. The mask of cunning that had always defined him, that sly intelligence that made smaller creatures nervous in his presence, was gone entirely. What remained was a diminished, fragile creature held together by little more than stubborn will and the instinct to keep moving forward.

Pity severed her paralysis. She moved to him without thought, closing the distance between them in swift strides and catching his weight as his balance finally faltered. His body felt lighter than it should have, as if pain had hollowed him out from within. She could feel the rapid flutter of his heart through his ribs, quick and shallow as a bird's.

"Come, rest a moment," she murmured, guiding him toward a break in the canopy where weak light pooled on the ground. Up close, his scent carried notes of rank musk mixed with wet iron, and something bitter that she recognized as crushed ferns and torn vegetation. Beneath it all lingered the acrid smell of fear-sweat. "Goodness, what happened? Are you alright?"

Mr. Fox attempted a smile, the ghost of his old sly grin that had unnerved so many market-goers, but pain swallowed it before it could fully form. His lips pulled back briefly, revealing teeth stained pink with blood. "Dogs," he said, the word scraping through his throat like gravel. "The hunter's dogs."

She eased him down against the base of an ancient cedar whose trunk was wide enough that ten rabbits holding paws couldn't encircle it. Its roots had pushed up through the ground over centuries, creating natural hollows and rises that now formed a cradle for his broken form. The bark was deeply furrowed, offering some small shelter from the rain. She crouched beside him and examined the wounds more closely, her stomach turning at what she found.

"Here, let me help," she said gently, though her paws trembled as she reached for the first thorn.

One by one, she worked them free. Each extraction produced a wet, sucking sound as barbs released their grip on flesh, followed by fresh wells of blood that rose to fill the wounds. The thorns themselves were monstrous things, not the delicate spikes of wild roses or the thin needles of hawthorn, but thicker, with jagged hooks at the base designed to embed and hold. Some were as long as her sewing needles, their tips stained dark with his blood. She laid each extracted thorn on a broad maple leaf beside them, forming a grim collection that grew with each removal.

As she worked, she murmured softly, a continuous stream of comforting sounds rather than distinct words. Her voice became a rhythm he could follow, something to focus on beyond the pain, and gradually his ragged breathing aligned with it. His eyes, which had been wide with shock, began to close. By the time she removed the final thorn from his haunch, Mr. Fox had gone pale beneath his russet fur, his eyelids fluttering with the effort of remaining conscious. Sweat beaded along his muzzle despite the cold rain.

She tore a strip from her dress hem. The material was good cotton, thick and absorbent, though she mourned its loss. She bound his injured foreleg tightly, using two slender cedar twigs as a makeshift splint to hold it in place. The fabric quickly bloomed with small red flowers where his blood seeped through.

Only when the makeshift splint was secured did she allow herself to breathe fully.

"Where is my husband?" she asked, her voice softer now but weighted with desperation. The question had been burning in her throat since she'd first recognized him. "Did they... did they catch him?" Her voice caught on the question, breaking slightly. Mrs. Rabbit reached into her pocket and drew out the bloodied scrap of fabric, holding it out for him to see. The tweed seemed to glow dully in the dim light, its stain dark as old wine.

Mr. Fox's eyes focused on the fabric with obvious effort. Recognition flickered across his features, followed by something that might have been relief. He closed his eyes briefly, gathering strength to speak. "He mentioned getting caught in a tangle of branches near the old fence line by the orchard. Said they scraped his arm badly and tore his scarf to pieces. But he was alive when I saw him last. Very much alive." He shifted against the root, a wince flashing across his features as the movement pulled at his wounds.

"I'd gone to market yesterday morning. Bought a sack of potatoes for winter storage from Mrs. Mole. Good ones too, firm and without blemish. On my way back, I passed the orchard and encountered Mr. Rabbit coming through the gates. We exchanged pleasantries, nothing important. Talk of the weather, the early frost we'd had. I mentioned having a few jars of wild strawberry jam left from my summer preserves. He's always been particularly fond of them, so I offered one."

His gaze found hers, clouded with pain but earnest. There was none of his usual slyness there, no hint of deception. "He offered to walk back with me, said he was in no particular hurry. When we reached my den, I went inside to wrap up the jam properly. Found an old piece of oilcloth to keep it safe. We talked a little longer while I worked, just idle chatter about the coming frost, whether the winter would be harsh. He mentioned you were planning to make a pie, he seemed eager to get back."

Relief nearly buckled her knees. She had to steady herself against the cedar trunk, its rough bark grounding her. A knot that had been tightening in her throat began to loosen. Mr. Rabbit might still be safe. She clung to that hope like a drowning creature grasps at reeds.

"He departed shortly after we arrived," Mr. Fox

continued, his voice growing stronger with the telling. "I watched him head back toward the orchard path. He seemed in good spirits when we parted."

Hope flickered through her, tentative as a match struck in wind. But doubt followed quickly, snuffing it out just as fast. Mr. Rabbit left unharmed. But he didn't come home. The two facts refused to reconcile in her mind. She studied Mr. Fox's face, searching for any sign of deception, but found only pain and exhaustion. Still, old suspicions died hard.

"And what about you?" she asked, gaze drifting once more over the wounds, his mangled leg, the filth ground deep into his coat. "How did this happen?"

Mr. Fox let his head rest against the tree, his eyes focusing on something beyond her shoulder, perhaps seeing the memory play out again. "After he left, I tidied up a bit, then decided to catch a trout for my supper. The jam had made me think of fish, how well they pair. Headed toward the south stream where the current slows around the bend, forms a nice deep pool where the big ones like to rest. The path there goes through a clearing I've used a hundred times. But the wind was against me, blowing from the east. I couldn't catch the dogs' scent until it was too late. Walked into that clearing, unaware they were already there, waiting."

He paused, jaw tightening with the memory. She could see his pulse jumping in his throat. "They came at me from three sides. Big brutes, not the local farm dogs but proper hunting hounds. Bred for the chase. I ran. No shame in admitting it. Managed to dive into a thicket of brambles that grows near the old stone wall. Vicious things with thorns thick as darning needles, but they formed a barrier between me and those slavering jaws.

The dogs stayed for hours, barking, baying, trying to find a way through. One of them, a spotted hound with a torn ear, kept circling, looking for weakness. But the hunters never appeared. I kept expecting to hear their horns, their voices, but nothing came. Eventually, I think the hounds grew bored of waiting. They loped back into the woods, following some other scent. I waited until morning before crawling out, then limped home... and found you standing in my path."

Mrs. Rabbit's paw found his shoulder, resting there gently. She could feel him trembling beneath her touch,

whether from cold or delayed shock she couldn't tell.
"You poor thing," she whispered. "I'm glad you were able
to get away. Those brambles saved your life."

The rain, which had been a gentle patter during their
conversation, now fell with renewed purpose. It gathered
in the folds of his fur, creating rivulets that carried away
grime and blood in pale pink streams. The wind had taken
on a knife-edge chill that cut through her coat, making
her suddenly aware of how cold they both must be. The
temperature had dropped noticeably since she'd left
home.

"Let me help you inside," she said, decision crystallizing.
"We need to get you warm and dry before you catch your
death."

The journey to his den, though visible from where they
sat as a dark opening in the hillside, seemed to stretch
endlessly. Each step became its own small ordeal. Mr. Fox
leaned heavily against her, his weight shifting with each
movement, threatening to topple them both. His
breathing came in thin wheezes punctuated by small
sounds of pain he tried to suppress. They passed beneath
a fallen log lodged into another tree, where shelf

mushrooms cascaded in rippled layers, their surfaces painted in bands of cream and rust. Mrs. Rabbit spared them only a glance before pressing onward, though part of her mind catalogued them automatically as turkey tail, good for medicinal tea.

His burrow entrance appeared as a dark mouth in the hillside, partially veiled by a curtain of trailing ivy that had grown thick over the years. The stone-lined opening exhaled cool, damp air that carried complex scents from within. As she guided him through the entrance, she had to duck her head, the opening sized for a fox's slinking approach rather than a rabbit's upright gait.

Inside, the scent of sweet preserves mingled with dried meat hanging from the rafters. Strings of sausages and what might have been dried fish formed dark silhouettes against the ceiling. Mrs. Rabbit tried not to dwell on where the meat had come from, though her nose detected nothing of rabbit among the preserved foods. Shelves carved directly into the earthen walls held rows of jars and bottles, their contents catching the weak glow of her lantern as she hung it from a hook by the door.

A bed tucked into an alcove, little more than a nest of

blankets and straw, offered Mr. Fox refuge. The bedding had seen better days, patched and re-patched until the original fabric was barely visible. She lowered him onto it carefully, mindful of his injuries, then retrieved a threadbare towel from a nearby shelf. The cloth was worn soft with use, more gray than its original white. She began gently drying his fur, each movement revealing new injuries hidden beneath dirt and matted hair: scratches that crisscrossed his flanks, bruises darkening beneath the fur of his ribs, a deep cut along his hip that had partially scabbed over.

A dented kettle sat atop a makeshift stove fashioned from an old iron barrel. The metal showed signs of many repairs, different metals creating a patchwork effect. She filled it with water from a clay jug, noting how he'd scratched tally marks into the clay, perhaps counting days or meals or something else entirely. While the water heated, she examined his collection of medicinal herbs arranged on a corner shelf. Her fingers moved with the practiced purpose of one who'd tended many wounds, selecting willow bark for pain, yarrow to slow bleeding, meadowsweet to reduce fever. She added a few leaves of feverfew for good measure, bundling them all into a small cloth pouch that she steeped in the heated water until it turned dark and fragrant. The aroma that rose from the cup was sharp and bitter, medicinal rather than pleasant, but she knew it would help.

She helped him drink it, supporting his head while he swallowed with obvious effort. His throat worked slowly, and she had to pause several times to let him catch his breath. The warmth seemed to help; color began returning to the pale skin visible inside his ears.

The stub of candle she lit on the windowsill cast elongated shadows across the rough walls, illuminating a collection of curious trinkets she hadn't noticed at first. A dried bat wing spread and pinned to a board like a butterfly, a rusted compass with its needle permanently fixed north, a tarnished locket on a broken chain. Books lined one wall, their spines faded and titles illegible. Outside, the wind moaned through the trees, a low, ceaseless keening that made the walls seem thinner than they were.

"I'm going to fetch Mr. Hedgehog," she said once Mr. Fox's breathing had deepened into the slow rhythm of exhausted sleep. His chest rose and fell steadily now, the tea already working its mild magic. "You need proper medicine beyond my simple remedies. He'll have something stronger for the pain, and herbs to prevent infection."

He managed a faint nod without opening his eyes. "Thank you, Mrs. Rabbit... please... be careful," he murmured, words already slurring with approaching sleep. "The dogs..." But whatever warning he intended was lost as consciousness slipped from him.

She tucked another blanket around his form, noting how small he looked in sleep, all his predatory presence dissolved. She made sure the fire in the stove was banked safely, then turned toward the door. Beyond the threshold, the sky had thickened into a solid sheet of iron-gray, trees writhing in the strengthening gale like tormented souls. She fastened her coat at the throat, checked that the buttons were secure, lifted the lantern from its hook, and set out on the path toward Mr. Hedgehog's apothecary.

Her footsteps fell into a steady rhythm against the packed earth, but her thoughts spun beneath it, looping through fragments of Mr. Fox's account. The timeline made sense, but gaps remained. Mr. Rabbit had gone somewhere after leaving the fox's den. He hadn't returned home. Perhaps he'd encountered the dogs later, after Mr. Fox had already been driven into the brambles.

Thunder rolled across the treetops like a giant's wagon wheels on cobblestones. She counted heartbeats between the sound and the distant flash, gauging the storm's approach by the old method her mother had taught her. Still far enough not to worry immediately, but not far enough to ignore. The rain continued to fall steadily.

She paused to catch her breath beside a fallen oak. White feathers clung to the bark in scattered clumps, evidence of some struggle. They were too large for songbirds, possibly from a goose. The electric charge in the air raised the fine hairs along her arms, making her fur stand on end despite her heavy coat. She quickened her pace.

Then came a sound behind her, soft at first, barely distinguishable from the rustling leaves.

She turned, half-expecting to see Mr. Fox having followed despite his injuries, but dismissed the thought immediately. He'd been fast asleep when she left, barely able to keep his eyes open.

"Hello?" she called. "Is someone there?"

No answer came. Yet the sound grew louder, a steady padding of heavy feet.

The underbrush parted like a curtain drawn aside. A shape moved toward her with terrible grace: sleek, low to the ground, purposeful in its approach. A hound emerged from between the trees, its outline sharp despite the rain. Its frame was gaunt but powerful, ribs visible beneath a rough, brindled coat streaked with soot and mud. The beast's head remained low, ears pricked forward like twin daggers, nostrils flaring wide as it caught her scent on the rain-washed air.

She took one slow step backward. Then another. Her heel caught on a root, nearly sending her sprawling, but she caught herself. The wind betrayed her then, shifting suddenly to carry her scent in a direct current toward the hound, rich with the smell of fear.

It froze. Lifted its muzzle skyward. Inhaled deeply, its chest expanding as it drew in her scent, cataloging, identifying, marking.

Its gaze dropped, steady and malevolent, and locked with hers. In those dark eyes, she saw no mercy, no recognition of her as anything but prey. For one suspended moment, neither moved. The world narrowed to just the two of them.

Then the dog lunged.

CHAPTER 6

Mrs. Rabbit dropped to all fours and ran, the lantern slipping from her grip and shattering against a stone. Glass burst into a thousand glittering shards, catching the flame's final light before it hissed out and vanished. She didn't dare look back. The sudden, profound darkness felt like a physical weight. Thought dissolved, replaced by a primal instinct that drove her claws into the forest floor, desperate for footing on the rain-slick earth.

Behind her, the hound's baying splintered the sleeping forest. Each howl reverberated off the tree trunks, transforming the single voice into a phantom pack that seemed to surround her from all sides. The sound was a tangible thing, a pressure against her ears. It bounced and multiplied until she could no longer tell if one dog pursued her, or a dozen. Her ears pinned flat against her skull as low-hanging branches whipped past her face, leaving stinging welts beneath her fur. The forest became a blur of brown and green, punctuated by the ghostly white flash of birch bark.

The ground slammed up to meet her with every stride, jarring her bones. Her paws and boots struck slick earth, each print a perfect impression, a clear signpost marking her path for the hound to follow. The rain had turned the leaf litter into a treacherous carpet that shifted and slid beneath her, threatening to send her sprawling. She jumped a fallen birch, its pale bark peeling away like bandages from an old wound to reveal the dark, rotting wood beneath. She landed harder than she intended. Her ankle twisted on a hidden stone, and a sharp, searing pain shot through the joint. A small cry escaped her lips, but she shoved the agony aside, compartmentalizing it.

She knew better than to double back toward the orchard or the familiar trails that led home. Her own scent was a map, and to follow it would be to lead the hound straight to the doorsteps of her friends. To lead it to Mr. Hedgehog, busy with his tinctures, or Mr. Squirrel, who would be barricaded in his drey—the thought of those jaws, that relentless hunger, finding them twisted her stomach with a dread that eclipsed her own fear. She veered sharply right, her body tilting so low her flank nearly grazed the mud, and plunged into a tract of woods she knew only by reputation. It was a place where paths unraveled, the very part of the forest young kits were always warned to stay away from. She had grown up on stories of lost travelers who were never seen again, and now she hoped that same confusing wilderness would be enough to lose the hound.

The character of the woods changed instantly. The air turned colder, the trees here grew in tormented shapes. Ancient hardwoods, their bark blackened and furrowed as if by some long-ago fire, twisted toward a sky they could not reach, their limbs gnarled like the arthritic hands of giants. Between them, younger trees grew in unnatural angles, contorting themselves in their struggle for a sliver of light. The undergrowth thickened into grasping walls of thorn and briar, forcing her to weave an erratic path that cost precious seconds. Sticky strands of caterpillar silk stretched between the branches, clinging to her whiskers and tangling in her eyelashes as she ran through them.

The hound's voice changed, drawing closer, its timber laced with a chilling certainty. Through the frantic drumming of her own heart, she could hear it close the distance—the loud shredding of undergrowth beneath its weight, the wet, rhythmic panting of its open mouth, the sharp scrape of its claws against a log as it vaulted over an obstacle that had nearly stopped her. A branch cracked like a rifle shot as the dog tested its jaws, practicing for the moment it would close around her spine. She could almost feel the predator's focus, the way it would be drinking in her scent, its entire world narrowed to her, its prey.

Her lungs burned with each gasping breath, furnaces of pain. The cold air felt like broken glass in her throat, offering no relief. Her vision began to tunnel, the edges of the world fraying and creeping into darkness until only a narrow corridor of escape remained ahead. Her world focused on the present: leap the root, dodge the stones, keep moving. The strange, dark beauty of this deep forest passed almost unnoticed: ghost-fungi painting the ground in their eerie, green light; bracket mushrooms that wept thick, crimson ooze the color of blood; and a sudden bloom of velvet-petaled flowers that blanketed the forest floor in hues of violet and indigo.

A rusted metal barb, sharp as a fishing hook, snagged her thigh as she burst through a hedge. It tore through her satchel strap, sending the bag tumbling from her shoulder. A second hook sliced through her coat, and she winced as it bit into her own flesh. Blood welled immediately, a shocking warmth against the cold air, and began to trickle down her leg. Each drop that fell to the forest floor was a betrayal, a scarlet marker for the hound's sensitive nose, one the steady rain could not wash away fast enough.

The deep baying of the hound broke, pitching into a series of frenzied yips of raw excitement. It wasted no time picking up her blood trail. The disciplined rhythm of the hunt dissolved, replaced by the ragged ecstatic breathing of a predator that knows its prey is wounded.

Panic constricted Mrs. Rabbit's chest. Her paw found a stone slimed with green algae and slipped again. She went down hard, her shoulder striking an exposed root with a force that sent a wave of jarring pain down every nerve in her arm. The impact drove the remaining air from her lungs in a silent scream. For one stunned moment, she lay in the mud, stars dancing before her eyes, her mind unable to process the fall. Then the sound of the hound crashing through the bracken—so close now, terrifyingly close—sent a current of pure adrenaline through her. She tore off her coat, the weight of the garment slowing her down, and scrambled to her feet, ignoring the throb in her shoulder, the mud caking her fur, the fire in her lungs.

Boughs drooped from the trees like gallows ropes. She ducked beneath them, sometimes dropping to her belly to wriggle under barriers too high to leap, the damp earth cold against her stomach. She pressed on, drawing on reserves of strength she hadn't known she possessed, the kind that surfaces only when death is quickly closing in.

Through the dizzying maze of trunks, she spotted it: a massive oak, felled by lightning or age, its core rotted away to form a dark, hollow maw in the side of the log. A refuge.

She dove for the gap without breaking stride. The entrance was narrower than it appeared, splintered wood scraping her back raw as she writhed into the hollow. The scent of decay flooded her nostrils, damp soil mingling with fungal spores and the bitter aroma of tannins leaching from decomposing wood. Bugs skittered deeper into the cavity at her intrusion. Clay, cool and undisturbed for years, packed beneath her claws. The space compressed around her until she could go no deeper, wedged in the dead, silent heart of the tree, where she could do nothing but wait and listen.

She removed her boots to ease the swelling in her ankle. Mrs. Rabbit forced her breathing to slow, though her lungs screamed for air. Without her wool coat, and with the heat from her run ebbing away, the autumn cold bit deep into her. An uncontrollable shiver seized her, and she clenched every muscle to still the violent trembling.

The forest fell utterly quiet. A single drop of water fell from the roof of her hiding place. *Tap.* The sound was impossibly loud. She counted the seconds until the next. *Tap.*

Then the silence shattered.

Claws scrabbled against the bark outside. The hound circled her sanctuary, its movements purposeful, testing the wood from every angle. A frustrated whine vibrated through the log, followed by a howl of pure, savage triumph. It knew exactly where she hid. Through a crack in the rotted wood, she watched it pace—a beast even larger than her worst imaginings, a gaunt engine of muscle. A healed scar split one ear, perhaps evidence of another prey that had fought for its life. The dog's eyes, dark and intelligent, were fixed on her hiding place.

It slammed into the tree, scattering rot and dirt onto her head. The hound's jaws locked onto a protruding branch thick as her arm, and with a savage twist of its neck, it tore the wood away. The crack of splintering timber sounded like breaking bones. It spat out the fragment and attacked again, tireless and methodical, dismantling her shelter piece by piece. Its hot breath, carrying the stench of flesh and the faint scent of human, steamed in the cool air and drifted through the gaps.

Mrs. Rabbit's paw fumbled in her pocket, closing around the familiar, smooth weight of the sewing needle. It felt absurdly small, a pathetic sliver against the teeth that were tearing their way toward her.

The dog tore away a final, large section of the log and thrust its muzzle into the opening. She saw it all with terrible clarity: the individual whiskers quivering with each breath, the strings of saliva hanging from its jaws, the pink gums pulled back from yellowed teeth. Its nose, black and wet, worked frantically, drinking in her scent. A low growl rumbled from its chest.

Time stretched thin. The hound gathered itself for the killing lunge, its eyes rolling back to show the whites in its bloodlust.

As the dog drove forward, Mrs. Rabbit plunged the needle into the soft cartilage of the hound's nose with all the strength terror had lent her.

It sank deep. The dog's yelp was so piercing that she quickly clamped her paws over her ears. The beast reeled backward, snapping at empty air, its paws clawing frantically at its own face. Blood sprayed across the leaves, the bark, her own fur. Its cries turned from predatory hunger to bewildered agony

She didn't wait. Scrambling backward, she burst from an opening on the far end of the tree and ran, leaving her boots behind. Her muscles, stiff from the brief rest, screamed in protest. Behind her, the dog's furious howls devolved into wet, choking whines and sneezes as it tried to clear the blood from its nostrils.

Mrs. Rabbit ran until her legs were numb, deeper into the forest, where the ground gave way to a carpet of moss glowing with phosphorescent light. Tears streamed down her face, blurring her vision. She began to laugh in short, erratic bursts, a hysterical tremor shaking her entire body. She nearly choked on her own spit, coughing uncontrollably between bouts of laughter. Her thoughts felt distant, unmoored, as though no longer fully her own.

Her pace faltered, finally overtaken by exhaustion. Her legs moved through will alone now, each step a shambling effort. Her ankle throbbed with a relentless, pulsing beat, the pain no longer possible to ignore.

Her delirious mind didn't register the disturbed earth ahead, the unnatural patch of bare soil amid the moss. She missed the way the dim light glinted off a sliver of dark metal, nearly hidden beneath a careful arrangement of leaves. If her vision hadn't been clouded by tears and rain, if her senses had still been sharp, she might have noticed the faint trace of a human scent nearby. Still running blindly, her paw landed on the disturbed patch. A metallic whine cut through the air as a wire snapped taut around her leg, brutally yanking her backward.

White-hot pain shot up from her ankle, ripping a scream from her throat and leaving it raw. For a moment, she could only stare at her leg in detached horror. The wire had bitten through her flesh, drawing a perfect circle of blood that welled up, dark against her fur. When she instinctively tried to pull away, the trap only tightened its grip, the wire sinking deeper into her flesh with an audible grating sound.

CHAPTER 7

The pain tore through Mrs. Rabbit's ankle, sharp and relentless. She twisted around to examine her leg, and dread rose in her chest at the sight of the wire biting deep into her flesh, blood seeping into the mud. The metal snare, deceptively thin, had tightened mercilessly around her ankle and was anchored firmly into the hard-packed earth. Every tiny movement sent fresh jolts of agony through her leg, leaving her breath ragged and shallow.

She forced herself to stay calm, though panic surged beneath her skin. Carefully, Mrs. Rabbit reached toward her ankle, but even the slightest touch made the wire dig deeper. She began clawing at the ground around the snare, desperate to unearth the stake anchoring it down. But the earth was packed tight, hardened by countless rains and dense with stubborn roots and stones. Her claws scraped uselessly against the unforgiving soil.

She pulled again, wrenching with all her strength, her shoulders trembling from the strain. The wire only tightened further, slicing deeper into muscle, drawing a raw cry of anguish and defeat from her throat. Exhausted, she collapsed into the mud, gasping for breath, her body shaking uncontrollably. The reality of her predicament settled around her like a crushing weight.

As a last, desperate thought, Mrs. Rabbit searched her pockets for the needle, the one small defense she'd carried from home. Her paws shook violently as she felt through the empty fabric, her heart sinking when she remembered leaving the needle embedded in the hound's nose. She had nothing left to protect herself — no way to defend against whatever might find her in the darkness.

Mrs. Rabbit dragged herself back until she felt the solid bark of a nearby tree pressing against her spine. She sagged against it, pressing a paw against her heart as if to steady its frantic rhythm. The rain continued to fall around her, pattering softly on leaves and dripping from the branches overhead. Through sparse gaps in the shifting, overcast sky, faint glimmers of starlight briefly appeared, pale and distant between the heavy clouds. Evening had settled over the forest, but traces of twilight lingered, tinting the world in muted shades of gray and blue.

Breathing heavily, Mrs. Rabbit stared upward at the clouds growing darker and denser. The thick, ominous shelf of storm clouds were nearly overhead, swallowing the remaining fragments of light beneath it. Soon, she knew the rain would worsen, and her chances of escape would vanish completely. Trapped and alone, she realized her time was running out.

Mrs. Rabbit's ears snapped to attention, picking up distant barking. Faint at first, the sound sharpened gradually, carving through the sound of falling rain. Her breath caught in her throat as she strained to listen, muscles tensed and trembling beneath her fur. Another bark, clearer this time, rang out. A man's voice followed — a shout muffled by distance, yet undeniably commanding.

Her heart quickened painfully. Fear rippled through her as she waited, vulnerable against the rough bark. But gradually, the barking faded and the man's voice diminished too. A shuddering breath escaped her lungs, her muscles releasing slightly as relief mingled with the lingering dread.

A dark shadow slid silently across the damp earth, drawing her attention upward. A vulture landed gracefully on a low, sturdy branch just beyond the clearing, its talons gripping tightly as the limb bobbed gently beneath its weight. It perched there quietly, feathers dark and sleek from the rain, its bald head tilting curiously to regard her. Its gaze settled on her trapped leg, then drifted slowly upward to meet her eyes, holding them without blinking, calm and patient and knowing.

A second bird joined the first, alighting noiselessly a few branches away, its broad wings barely disturbing the air. Two more soon followed, quietly claiming perches nearby. None of them made a sound. Their bodies were hunched slightly, feathers heavy and glistening with rain, their eyes black and intent. After a moment, one bird extended its wings fully, droplets cascading silently from dark feathers as it stretched. It held the posture briefly— wings open wide, their span impressive and unsettling— then folded them again, shaking its head briskly, water dripping from its hooked beak.

Mrs. Rabbit watched, throat tight with anxiety, as the vultures settled into a quiet vigil. Their gazes never wandered, never wavered; each pair of eyes fixed steadily upon her, calmly marking time.

Mrs. Rabbit's eyelids fluttered, drifting in and out of
consciousness, her mind slipping into fragments of
memories as the steady patter of rain faded into distant
murmurs. The cold of the forest floor receded, giving way
to a gentle rocking beneath her. A different sound
emerged softly from the depths of her mind—the
rhythmic creak of wooden oars moving through still
water.

She was sitting in a small wooden boat, crafted carefully
by Mr. Rabbit's patient paws. It glided across the calm
surface of a pond near his grandmother's farm, cutting
effortlessly through patches of floating lily pads and
clusters of pale blossoms. Warm sunlight spilled
generously from a bright and cloudless sky, caressing her
fur until it grew pleasantly hot, sinking gently into her
skin. Her cheeks flushed softly beneath the golden
warmth.

Between them rested a small wicker picnic basket, packed
neatly with cucumber sandwiches and a glass jar of
wildflower tea sweetened lightly with honey. She recalled
the delicate taste of the sandwiches, crisp and refreshing,

and the faintly floral tea, cool and soothing against her tongue.

Across from her, Mr. Rabbit rowed steadily, his paws gripping the smooth wooden handles of the oars, guiding the boat gracefully along the pond's edge. He sang quietly —a gentle melody with words she couldn't quite remember now, though she could still feel the comforting lilt of his voice, steady and clear. Sunlight caught in the soft chestnut fur of his cheeks and brightened the flecks of gold in his eyes.

A rumble of thunder rolled through the clouds, shaking the earth beneath Mrs. Rabbit and pulling her sharply back into awareness. Her eyes blinked open, the comforting warmth of her memory fading.

Something moved behind a dense cluster of brush just beyond her sight. She stiffened, ears twitching slightly, as she strained to listen. Footsteps were weaving slowly through the thick underbrush. Each step sent another shiver of fear rippling through her body. Mrs. Rabbit pressed her back tighter to the tree.

She glanced upward at the vultures. Three still watched

her without shifting, but one had turned its attention toward the rustling brush, its head tilted intently, waiting.

Then, at the edge of her vision, something appeared above the tangled greenery. A pair of rabbit ears, tall and unmistakably familiar, emerged into view. She stared, blinking rapidly, certain that exhaustion and loss of blood had finally broken her senses. The rain blurred her vision, and she lifted a trembling paw to brush it from her eyes. Yet the ears remained there, clearly outlined against the dull sky.

A moment later, Mr. Rabbit stepped quietly into the open. He paused at the edge of the clearing, shoulders relaxed, eyes warm and focused solely on her. He still wore his black coat, its top button left open just as he had worn it that morning. But this time she noticed the button was missing, leaving a small, frayed hole in the fabric.

He took her in quietly, calmly, before beginning to move toward her. As he stepped closer, she realized there was something different about him, something impossible: a faint, pale light seemed to cling to his fur, illuminating him softly against the deepening shadows of the trees.

Mrs. Rabbit stared at him, her vision wavering through a fresh swell of tears, hot and bewildered as they slid freely down her face. She didn't dare move, or breathe, or speak, afraid the smallest movement might break the fragile moment and prove it wasn't real.

As Mr. Rabbit moved toward her, a smile spread across his familiar face. It was the same tender expression he'd worn countless times, steadying her through every difficulty. That smile alone banished all lingering fears, washing away every doubt and pain until only he remained, walking steadily across the damp forest floor.

Mrs. Rabbit's chest swelled with relief and joy so powerful it nearly overwhelmed her. Her paws instinctively reached out toward him, desperate to hold him, to feel the reassuring solidity of his presence. She had come searching for Mr. Rabbit, but instead, he had found her. They could finally go home.

As he stepped closer, she saw the faint misty glow enveloping him more clearly now, a soft, silvery fog clinging gently to his fur. Her vision tunneled, completely focused on the warmth of his eyes and the certainty in his smile.

She smiled back at him, joy lighting her face as brightly as the strange, gentle illumination that surrounded him.

"Hello, love," Mr. Rabbit said softly, his voice warm and comforting as he knelt before her, reaching out to grasp her trembling paws gently in his own.

His touch was firm, reassuring, his paws just as she remembered them—worn and familiar from years of tending their home and garden. She could not form words; they tangled in her throat, caught in a sob of relief. Her body shivered, emotions overwhelming her senses. She leaned instinctively toward him.

Mr. Rabbit moved closer still, leaning forward to press his nose softly against hers in a familiar gesture they'd shared countless times. Mrs. Rabbit closed her eyes, savoring the sweetness of that tender moment. But the instant their noses touched, a chill ran sharply through her body. His nose was ice-cold, so deeply and profoundly cold it startled her.

Her eyes flew open, and she recoiled instantly, a startled gasp escaping her throat. Mr. Rabbit still knelt before her, yet something had shifted horribly in his appearance. His clothing, which moments ago had seemed tidy despite its missing button, was now frayed and disheveled, stained by dirt and dark patches of dampness. His fur, previously rich and lustrous, now appeared faded to a sickly, grayish brown, patchy and unkempt as if decaying.

Worst of all were his eyes. They had become deeply sunken, hollow and distant, staring through her rather than at her, empty of recognition. Mrs. Rabbit stared back in shock, unable to comprehend what she saw.

"It's too late," Mr. Rabbit whispered softly, his voice brittle.

Mrs. Rabbit shook her head. "What's too late...?" she began to ask, her voice cracking with confusion and fear.

But before she could finish her sentence, a sudden, blinding flash of lightning ripped across the sky, illuminating the entire forest in stark, harsh brilliance. Mrs. Rabbit instinctively shielded her eyes, the brightness so intense it left vivid afterimages burning into her vision.

A massive clap of thunder followed immediately, the sound deafening, rattling through the trees. It was deep and resonant, declaring unmistakably that the storm had arrived in full force, heavy and merciless.

As the echoing thunder faded into silence, Mrs. Rabbit's eyes slowly adjusted again. When she looked forward, Mr. Rabbit was gone. Nothing remained of him but empty space, the spot where he knelt now vacant as though he had never been there at all.

A sudden flurry of motion drew her attention upward. The vultures had taken flight, launching silently and simultaneously from their perches. Their large wings stretched wide, catching the wind effortlessly, rising together into the storm-darkened sky. She watched them, bewildered, as they quickly vanished into the clouds overhead.

Mrs. Rabbit's eyes snapped downward, drawn by another movement at the edge of her vision. Standing exactly where Mr. Rabbit had emerged moments earlier was now a small figure. It remained unmoving, silhouetted softly against the trees. As Mrs. Rabbit's sight finally cleared from the remnants of the blinding lightning, she saw it clearly for what it was—a child. Her expression was calm and unreadable, her wide eyes fixed firmly and curiously upon Mrs. Rabbit.

"Hello," said the little girl.

CHAPTER 8

Mrs. Rabbit stared at the girl. The wind picked up with a sudden howl, making the high branches creak. The sky was split by another jagged fork of lightning. She could hear the heavy drumming of rain falling in the nearby tree canopy, inching closer.

The child's black hair fell in layers around a heart-shaped face, the ends curving inward toward pale cheeks flushed pink from cold. She wore a yellow and white pinstriped dress beneath a sage green rain jacket too large for her shoulders, the fabric hanging loose at her waist. The sleeves had been rolled several times to free her hands, creating thick cuffs. Scuffed matching boots peeked from beneath her hem, the leather cracked and worn at the toes, mud caked in the creases. White bows, limp from moisture, clung to either side of her head, the ribbon edges frayed.

Mrs. Rabbit's mind struggled to make sense of what she was seeing. Her nose twitched, catching the smell of chamomile soap on the girl.

As the child stepped closer, her boots squelching softly in the mud, Mrs. Rabbit's gaze sharpened. Stains clung to her white stockings in uneven patches. A seam unraveled at the edge of her jacket pocket, the thread hanging loose and swaying.

"Oh," the girl said softly, her voice carrying the clear, bell-like quality that belonged only to the very young. "I've never seen a black rabbit before."

The words hung in the air between them. Mrs. Rabbit's throat constricted, her mouth suddenly dry despite the humid air. "Please," she managed, the word scraping past her lips. "I need help."

But the girl's face showed no recognition that Mrs. Rabbit had spoken. Her green eyes widened as they fixed on the wire snare that bit into Mrs. Rabbit's ankle. The metal had cut through flesh and muscle, leaving white bone visible beneath.

"You poor thing," she murmured, approaching with
deliberate slowness. Her voice carried genuine concern.
"Look at your foot! It's all bloody! Here, I can set it free."

Mrs. Rabbit remained frozen as the child knelt beside her,
the warmth of her body creating a small pocket of heat in
the chilling air. Her fingers—small but surprisingly deft—
worked at the mechanism, the metal cold and slick with
blood. She muttered half-formed reassurances, her tongue
poking out slightly in concentration.

When the wire snare finally released with a sharp click,
Mrs. Rabbit's body tensed against fresh pain. Blood
rushed back to deprived tissue, bringing a thousand
pinpricks of sensation. The girl cradled the injured limb
with unexpected gentleness.

"Oh, you're really hurt," the girl observed, her voice
dropping to a whisper that barely rose above the wind.
"Might be broken. That's not good at all. But don't
worry, I'll take care of you!"

Before Mrs. Rabbit could respond, the child gathered her
up with surprising strength. The movement sent a jolt of
agony through her injured leg. The girl quickly adjusted

her hold, creating a cradle with her arms where Mrs. Rabbit's weight distributed evenly. Her jacket was rough against Mrs. Rabbit's fur, the waterproof fabric crinkling with each step.

Mrs. Rabbit's thoughts turned to Mr. Rabbit, and with them came a pain far sharper than her physical injury. She couldn't make sense of what she had seen. Whether it was blood loss making her dizzy or a memory taking shape, she didn't know. The uncertainty gnawed at her.

The girl walked with confidence, her rubber boots making soft sucking sounds against the wet earth. She followed a trail Mrs. Rabbit hadn't noticed before—a path much wider than the narrow animal tracks she knew, its borders marked by stones worn smooth with age. Thin roots crossed the ground, exposed by countless passing feet. This was a human path, old and well-used.

The forest opened gradually, trees thinning as they approached a clearing. The girl hummed as she walked, broken occasionally by mindless chatter. "Almost there... didn't know there were wild black rabbits... got to you just in time, before the storm worsened..."

The wind carried new scents—woodsmoke and chickens. The smell of their musty feathers and droppings unmistakable.

The trees parted completely, revealing a cabin nestled in the clearing's center. Its walls were constructed of rough-hewn logs stained nearly black, each one fitted tightly against the next with thin lines of pale chinking between. Some chinking had crumbled, leaving gaps. A steep-pitched roof rose to a stone chimney from which smoke emerged, pale gray against dark sky. The column rose straight before wind caught it, stretching it into ghostly tendrils that dissolved among treetops.

Wooden steps led to a narrow porch where three chairs sat angled toward each other, a small table between them. Two chairs were larger, with arms worn smooth. The third, smaller and painted yellow, rocked gently in the wind, its rockers creaking against the boards. A lantern hung from a ceiling hook, illuminating the front door, its flame dancing and casting wavering shadows.

Windows glowed with warm light that spilled onto the porch. Through glass panes divided by wooden muntins, shapes moved—shadows passing back and forth.

Someone else was inside, their movements quick. A pot clanged.

A chicken coop sat near the house front, constructed of weathered boards and chicken wire that had rusted orange in places. The structure leaned slightly. Hens clucked softly inside, already settled on their roosts for the night. The yard held rows of garden beds bordered by split logs, vegetables at varying growth stages pushing up through dark soil. Tomato plants heavy with ripe fruit leaned against wooden stakes. Bean vines climbed strings. Squash leaves collected raindrops. It reminded Mrs. Rabbit of her own garden, though this one was larger and more carefully arranged, each row perfectly straight.

Instead of approaching the front door, the girl carried her around the cabin's side, following a narrow path of flat stones set into earth. They passed a woodpile stacked nearly to the eaves. The sweet scent of seasoned oak and maple logs filled Mrs. Rabbit's nostrils. An axe stood embedded in a chopping block, its blade gleaming.

A rain barrel sat nearby, its surface still and reflective as dark glass. Water bugs skated across. Beside it, late asters clung to life, purple petals closed tight. Weeds encroached at the edges.

Behind the cabin stood a structure that made Mrs. Rabbit's fur bristle with unease. The shed was a quarter the cabin's size, constructed of vertical planks weathered gray. Unlike the cabin's warm windows, the shed's glass panes were clouded with dust and grime, some cracked in spider patterns. Whatever lay within remained obscured. The single door hung slightly askew on its hinges, the bottom edge having carved an arc in the dirt. A padlock hung open from the latch, rust freckling its surface.

Rain fell in a sudden torrent, bringing the storm that had been gathering all evening just as they reached the shed door. Water began running in small rivers.

The girl hurried the last steps, boots splashing through puddles. She nudged the shed door open with her foot. Hinges protested with a long creak.

Inside, the girl lit a few candles, bringing to view a child's room that had taken root in a space designed for tools and machinery. Near the window sat a low table surrounded by small wooden chairs, their paint chipped and peeling in strips. Crayons and paper scraps scattered across the surface, wax shavings ground into wood grain. Some drawings lay half-finished. A cup of water for painting had evaporated, leaving dried pigment.

The wall above displayed drawings tacked up with bent nails and rusted thumbtacks. Some showed gardens with bright flowers. Butterflies with rainbow wings. But others depicted animals with black scribbled eyes, too many limbs sprouting from twisted bodies, or mouths sewn shut with thick lines. To the side, a dried snake had been nailed to wooden paneling, its split tongue lolled uselessly, empty sockets where eyes had been.

A worn stuffed bear rested on one chair, fur balding in patches. One button eye missing, the remaining eye hung loose. Shelves built from rough planks held dolls with cracked porcelain faces. Their dresses were stiff with brownish stains, some dolls missing limbs.

Garden tools leaned against furniture as if left mid-task. Shears and spades with handles darkened from use rested alongside hand-sewing needles far too large for cloth.

The air held competing scents that burned Mrs. Rabbit's nose. Garden supplies—fertilizer and pesticide mixed

with musty toys. But underneath, laced through
everything, was a sterile chemical smell. Mrs. Rabbit
caught sharp vinegar, the sting of formaldehyde making
her eyes water.

The girl seemed entirely comfortable in this space. She set
Mrs. Rabbit gently on a wooden table, its surface worn
smooth and draped in lace doilies. Mrs. Rabbit's injured
leg throbbed anew.

Her gaze wandered to another door set into the far wall,
smaller than the entrance. It stood open just a crack, soft
light spilling through. She couldn't see inside, but
shadows moved across the light. The girl noticed her
looking and walked quickly to the door, pushing it shut
with force. She took an old brass key from a hook and
turned it in the lock, then hung the key back where it
swayed.

The child returned to Mrs. Rabbit's side, opening a
drawer beneath the table and removing a small tin box.
Inside lay bandages, jars, and tools arranged with
surprising orderliness. She selected a cloth, dampened it
from a small pitcher, and began cleaning blood from Mrs.
Rabbit's leg.

"You're lucky I found you," the girl said conversationally. "Those traps can do awful damage to little things like you." Her hands moved with efficiency, applying salve that smelled of mint. It burned at first, making Mrs. Rabbit flinch, then numbed. "Don't worry though. It doesn't seem broken, just sprained. You'll heal fine."

Mrs. Rabbit watched the child work, torn between gratitude for her care and growing unease about her surroundings. The girl's hands were steady, her touch light where needed. A warning itch lingered at the back of Mrs. Rabbit's mind, but she didn't know much about human ways.

Rain drummed against the tin roof like tiny hammers. Water leaked through one corner into a bucket. Outside, the world had gone fully dark, broken only by occasional lightning flashes.

"There," the girl announced, securing a bandage with a small knot. "All finished. You can rest now."

She moved to a cupboard, withdrew soft fabric bundles, and arranged them in a doll's cradle. With the same gentle hands, she lifted Mrs. Rabbit and placed her on this makeshift bed, tucking small blankets around her, propping the injured leg on rolled cloth for elevation. "I'll come check on you in the morning," the girl said.

Mrs. Rabbit tried to speak, though she knew the child couldn't understand. She needed to leave, to continue searching for Mr. Rabbit. But before she could make any sound, noise from outside froze her mid-breath.

Barking.

A voice followed, deep and resonant, calling from the cabin's direction. "Ethel!"

The girl spun toward the door, face transforming with delight, eyes bright with excitement. "Oh! My pa is back home from hunting!" she exclaimed, clasping her hands together. "I'll be back in the morning, little rabbit. You just stay right here and get some sleep."

She hurried to the door, pausing only to look back once with a reassuring smile before slipping outside. The door closed with a gentle thud.

Mrs. Rabbit heard the soft click of a lock latching shut.

CHAPTER 9

Mrs. Rabbit's ankle throbbed throughout the night, heat radiated from the wound, spreading up her leg in waves. The shed's damp air pressed against her, making it hard to breathe.

Exhaustion pulled her into restless sleep where she drifted through fevered dreams. Mr. Rabbit knelt before her, his hazel eyes sunken into hollows, mouth soundlessly repeating *it's too late.* His smile stretched wider than normal, revealing rows of teeth that gleamed like porcelain shards.

The shed creaked in the wind, timbers groaning under pressure. Something scratched inside the walls—tiny claws against wood, the scurrying of rats seeking shelter from the storm.

When dawn's pale light slipped in through the window, painting thin stripes across the dirt floor, she stirred. Her muscles had stiffened during the night, each movement sending fresh aches through her body. For one delirious moment, her mind conjured the weight of her quilt, the familiar depression where Mr. Rabbit's body had rested beside her.

Reality returned with cruel precision.

Her blanket was patchwork rags stitched together with uneven seams. The pillow beneath her head reeked of soil and copper pennies, its stuffing lumpy and damp. Her injured leg had purple bruising visible at the bandage edges where fur had been matted down. The trap's phantom pressure remained.

Mrs. Rabbit tried to sit up. The movement sent the shed spinning. Dizziness washed over her in nauseating waves, bile rising hot and bitter in her throat. She gripped the edge of the bed, knuckles white beneath her fur, and held perfectly still until the sensation passed. Her breathing came shallow and quick through her nose.

Mrs. Rabbit surveyed the shed in morning light. The

space was larger than she'd initially thought in her pain-addled state. Walls sloped inward as they rose, narrowing toward a peaked roof. Shelves lined every vertical surface with a child's peculiar sense of order—jars of buttons sorted meticulously by color sat alongside cruel metal implements whose purpose Mrs. Rabbit didn't care to guess. The buttons caught the light, winking like eyes.

Small skulls, bleached white and polished to an unnatural shine, hung as wind chimes from the ceiling beams. They clinked together softly in the draft that seeped through gaps in the walls. Each skull bore tiny painted flowers on its surface—delicate roses and daisies rendered in fading pastels. A collection of doll heads perched on the highest shelf, their porcelain faces spider-webbed with cracks, glass eyes clouded and reflecting nothing back. Some had lost their hair, leaving only glue residue and tiny holes where strands had once been rooted.

Dust motes danced in the thin sunbeams, swirling in patterns. The light brought no warmth to the stale air, which hung thick with mildew and the lingering tang of chemicals. A workbench occupied one corner, its surface stained dark. Tools hung from pegs above it: tiny saws, needles of various sizes, spools of thread in colors that matched no natural fiber.

Mrs. Rabbit wrapped the ragged blanket tighter around her shoulders, but the chill had settled into her bones during the night. Her teeth chattered despite her efforts to still them.

She eased her legs over the bed's edge onto the wood table. The cold shot up through her paw pads. Testing her weight, she pressed down gently. Her ankle responded with sharp, immediate protest—a bolt of pain that traveled up her leg and into her hip. She pulled back, breathing hard through her nose, nostrils flaring with each exhale.

Hours crawled by with agonizing slowness. The window's rectangle of light slid across the floor, marking time like a sundial. She watched it move from one side of the shed to the other, counting the minutes in its progression. Outside, only occasional bird calls and branches rustling against the roof broke the oppressive silence.

Her stomach cramped with hunger. She hadn't eaten since she left to search for Mr. Rabbit. Time had become elastic in this place, stretching and compressing without logic. She pressed a paw to her middle, feeling the hollow ache beneath her ribs.

The latch scraped just after midday, metal grinding against metal.

Mrs. Rabbit tensed, every muscle coiling. Her ears swiveled toward the sound, tracking each scrape and click as someone worked the mechanism from outside. The door hinges groaned again as they yielded to pressure, the wood swollen with moisture from the night's rain. Light spilled across packed earth, harsh and blinding after hours spent in dimness. She squinted against it, eyes watering.

The girl's silhouette appeared black against the brightness, small and slight. She stood in the doorway for a long moment, head cocked as if listening to something before stepping inside.

She entered barefoot despite the cold ground, her toes caked with fresh earth that left dark prints across the floor. She wore a yellow dress with tiny embroidered flowers along the hem. In her hands, she balanced a chipped porcelain doll's bowl and matching floral plate. Water had sloshed over the bowl's edge, leaving a trail down her wrist.

The plate held shredded carrots forming a perfect circle around the edge, fresh lettuce leaves layered in the center like green roses, and a single slice of eggplant cut into a star shape and placed precisely in the middle.

The girl's face showed no emotion as she approached.

She sat cross-legged on a stool before Mrs. Rabbit without ceremony and set the plate down on the table between them. Only then did her expression shift, her lips curved into a smile.

"You must be hungry," she said, voice soft with barely contained excitement. "I picked these special for you. From mama's garden. She doesn't know."

Mrs. Rabbit remained perfectly still, not even her whiskers twitching, as the girl reached for her injured leg. The child's hands were small but sure, unwinding the bandage. The fabric stuck in places where blood had dried, and she worked it free with patient tugs. Each pull sent fresh sparks of pain up Mrs. Rabbit's leg, but she didn't flinch.

The wound beneath had begun closing, the angry red line now puckered and dark but no longer weeping clear fluid. The puncture marks from the trap's teeth were still visible —a perfect row of holes that had scabbed over but would likely scar.

The girl clicked her tongue against her teeth three times— observational, like a scientist examining a specimen. From her dress pocket, she withdrew a small tin no bigger than her palm. When she unscrewed the lid, a sharp medicinal scent flooded the air—pine resin and willow bark layered over something more acrid. The ointment inside was thick and gray-green, with bits of plant matter suspended in the base.

She scooped a generous amount onto two fingers and began applying it to the wound with circular dabs. The substance stung sharp as nettles, then shifted to a deep cooling sensation that numbed the worst of the throbbing pain. It was stronger than the mint-scented paste she had used the night before. The girl's face remained serene as she worked, humming under her breath. It reminded Mrs. Rabbit of Mr. Rabbit, but it brought her no comfort.

"Poor thing," she whispered, her breath carrying the scent

of peaches. "Found you just in time, didn't I? Those traps are terrible business..." She trailed off, focusing on her work.

She produced a fresh bandage from another pocket—clean white linen that smelled of lye soap—and rewrapped the leg. Her small fingers tucked the ends with surprising neatness, creating a secure binding that wouldn't slip. Throughout the process, Mrs. Rabbit watched the girl's face, searching for clues in those strange, unblinking green eyes.

When she finished, she sat back and smiled again. This time it seemed genuine, reaching her eyes and crinkling their corners. "There. All better. Well, getting better."

Mrs. Rabbit's stomach chose that moment to growl audibly. The sound seemed to delight the girl, who clapped her hands together once.

"Oh! You need to eat to get strong." She pushed the plate closer.

Mrs. Rabbit reached for a carrot strip with a trembling paw. Hunger had roared back to life, gnawing at her insides with sharp teeth. The carrot was sweeter than she expected, its flavor bright and clean. It had been pulled from the earth recently—she could taste the soil still clinging to its skin despite the washing. The lettuce was crisp, beaded with water droplets. The eggplant left a bitter aftertaste on her tongue that lingered unpleasantly.

The girl watched her eat with rapt attention, leaning forward slightly, her hands folded in her lap. She didn't blink, didn't look away, barely seemed to breathe. When Mrs. Rabbit had finished half the plate, the girl finally stood up.

"I have to go back to the house now," she announced, rising to her feet in one smooth motion. "Pa needs help washing the ticks off the hounds. They get so many in the tall grass. Fat ones, full of blood." She wrinkled her nose at the thought.

She gathered the old bandages and tucked them into her pocket, then picked up the bowl of water and set it within Mrs. Rabbit's reach. At the door, she paused, one hand on the frame, and looked back over her shoulder.

"I'll make you better soon," she promised. The words

should have been comforting, but something in her tone made Mrs. Rabbit's fur stand on end all along her spine.

The door closed with a soft click. The latch scraped back into place.

Days blurred together in the dim confines of the shed, marked only by the girl's visits and the slow progression of light across the floor. She came twice daily with clockwork precision—once in the morning with food, once in the evening with fresh bandages or water. The meals varied little: always vegetables, always arranged with the same obsessive care, always watched over with that unblinking stare.

Once, she arrived with neither food nor supplies, but merely to show Mrs. Rabbit a tiny skull—a baby mole's, she explained with pride. Its teeth were still intact, tiny white needles set in delicate jaw bones. She had painted miniature flowers on this one too, forget-me-nots in blue so pale they were almost white.

"I found it under the porch," she said, turning it over in her palms. "Already clean. The ants did all the work." She held it up to the light, admiring how the sun shone through the thinner parts of the bone. "Would you like one? I could paint rabbits on it instead of flowers."

Mrs. Rabbit had declined by simply shaking her head.

On the third day, the girl brought a silver-backed hairbrush with soft bristles and spent over an hour working through the tangles in Mrs. Rabbit's fur. She started at the tips and worked her way up to the roots, careful not to pull too hard. Her touch was surprisingly gentle, but her eyes never quite focused on what she was doing. They stared at some point slightly beyond Mrs. Rabbit.

"Pa says I spend too much time in here," she said, her voice taking on a dreamy quality. "But I like playing with my dolls. He just doesn't understand."

The brush stilled against Mrs. Rabbit's shoulder. Mrs. Rabbit's heart quickened as the girl's gaze suddenly sharpened, fixing directly on her eyes with uncomfortable intensity.

"But you're different." She resumed brushing with long, smooth strokes. "You're special. I can tell. You understand me, don't you? Not like my other stupid dolls. They just sit there."

She leaned closer, close enough that Mrs. Rabbit could see her pulse fluttering in her throat. Her breath was warm against Mrs. Rabbit's ear.

"You're going to be my favorite," she whispered, voice dropping to barely above a breath. "My little black rabbit. We'll have tea parties. I'll make you pretty dresses. You won't ever want to leave."

The last words carried a weight that pressed down on Mrs. Rabbit's chest, making it hard to breathe.

On the fourth night, long after the girl had latched the door behind her, Mrs. Rabbit tested her injured leg again. The pain had receded from sharp agony to a deep, dull ache—present but manageable. She gripped the edge of the doll's bed and stood slowly, carefully, distributing her weight to favor her good side.

The leg held.

She took one tentative step, then another. The wooden

table creaked beneath her weight but supported her. She limped slowly to the other end of the table, one paw trailing along the wall for balance. With each circuit, her stride grew more confident, though never completely without pain.

By the fifth day, she knew with crystal clarity that she had to leave. The forest beyond these walls was dangerous but she needed to find Mr. Rabbit. She needed to find her way home.

On the sixth morning, the familiar scrape of the latch announced the girl's arrival.

Mrs. Rabbit stood waiting at the center of the table. Her dress pockets bulged slightly with leftovers she had hidden from each meal.

The girl entered barefoot as she always did. In her hands, she carried a wooden bowl brimming with aromatic herbs —parsley and dill from the smell.

The sight of Mrs. Rabbit upright stopped her at the threshold as surely as if she'd walked into a wall. Her small body went completely rigid. The bowl slipped from her fingers and crashed to the floor with a clatter, scattering its contents across the packed dirt. The herbs scattered like green confetti.

For a long moment, neither of them moved. The morning sun slanted through the doorway, catching the dust motes stirred up by the bowl's impact.

"You naughty rabbit!" the girl finally exclaimed, her voice tight with annoyance. She huffed out a breath that stirred the loose hairs around her face. "You're not supposed to be up yet. You're still hurt."

Mrs. Rabbit took a careful step forward, both paws raised in what she hoped was a placating gesture. She pointed toward the door, then to herself, then to the forest beyond—a silent explanation of her intent. Her whiskers twitched with nervous energy.

The girl's small fists clenched at her sides, knuckles white with pressure. Her face flushed crimson from neck to hairline, then drained to a bloodless white so pale her freckles stood out like ink spots. She stomped one foot hard enough to rattle the dolls on their shelves. The skulls chimed together softly.

"I wasn't ready!" she wailed, the words torn from her throat with equal parts rage and despair. Her eyes filled with tears that trembled on her lashes.

Mrs. Rabbit took another careful step, this one angled toward the door. Her gaze never left the girl's face. In the span of seconds, the child's features shifted from anger back to a blank expression.

The tears vanished. The trembling lips stilled into a thin line. Her breathing slowed from rapid pants to slow inhales. She straightened her spine, chin lifted.

"It's okay," she said, her voice now light and sugary. "You just wanted to play."

Mrs. Rabbit felt every hair along her neck rise. She moved toward the door in careful steps. The open doorway beckoned, freedom just beyond its frame.

The girl stood perfectly still near the door. Her eyes had gone wide, pupils dilated despite the morning light.

Mrs. Rabbit edged closer to the door. One step. Another. Her trembling paw extended slowly toward the iron

handle, balancing on her strong foot as she leaned from
the table.

The girl suddenly sprang forward.

In one fluid motion, she scooped Mrs. Rabbit off her feet.
Her fingers locked around her middle, squeezing tight
enough to force the air from Mrs. Rabbit's lungs in a
painful wheeze. Mrs. Rabbit thrashed and kicked,
struggling against the unyielding grasp. Her claws
scrabbled uselessly at the girl's wrists.

The child didn't flinch at the scratches. Didn't loosen her
grip even slightly. Instead, she brought Mrs. Rabbit's face
close to her own, so close their noses nearly touched.

"No, little rabbit," she whispered, breath hot against Mrs.
Rabbit's face. "You're not allowed to leave. You're still
hurt."

Mrs. Rabbit went completely still.

"Tsk, tsk, tsk." The girl clucked her tongue, her head
tilting at an unnatural angle as she carried Mrs. Rabbit
across the room.

She approached a tall wooden crate tucked in the far corner of the shed, partially hidden behind a moth-eaten curtain. With her knee, she nudged the fabric aside. Still holding Mrs. Rabbit, she flipped the lid open with her free hand.

The interior revealed an assortment of small wire cages and wooden boxes fitted with tiny air holes. The girl reached in and selected a black wire cage, its metal rusted at the corners and along the joints. It was just large enough for a creature of Mrs. Rabbit's size.

She placed the cage on the wooden table with a metallic clang, unlatched its door, and dropped Mrs. Rabbit inside without ceremony. Mrs. Rabbit's injured leg hit the wired floor hard, sending a fresh spike of pain through her body. The door swung shut with a heavy click that reverberated through the wire. The latch twisted into place, metal scraping against metal with finality.

From within her new prison, Mrs. Rabbit watched the girl's face transform once more. The blank mask melted away, replaced by an expression of pure, radiant delight. Her cheeks flushed pink with excitement, and her eyes sparkled with a fevered light.

"Now," the girl said cheerfully, smoothing her dress with small, satisfied pats, "are you ready for your makeover?"

She clasped her hands together beneath her chin and bounced on her toes.

"I'm going to turn you into such a lovely doll. The very best one. You'll see—you'll be perfect when I'm done."

CHAPTER 10

Mrs. Rabbit woke the next morning before dawn, her body pressed against the corroded floor of the cage.

Her mouth was dry. She hadn't had anything to drink since the morning before. The little girl had left her in the cage and never returned with food or water. Her tongue stuck to the roof of her mouth, thick and swollen. Each attempt to swallow scraped her throat. The taste of metal from the cage bars lingered on her lips where she'd pressed her face against them in sleep.

She shifted, trying to find relief from the wire that had left a pattern of ridges across her flesh. No matter how she positioned herself, the metal grid pressed into her spine, her hips, her shoulders. The cage was too small to stretch fully, too narrow to turn without scraping against the sides. She gathered the rough scraps of fabric that were left in the cage and wedged them beneath her hip where the wire dug deepest.

The thin blanket she'd been given was damp with night sweat. It clung to her fur in uncomfortable patches, too small to cover her completely.

In the far corner of the shed, a curtain of burlap hung from the rafters. It stirred without any breeze to move it. Dust drifted down in a fine shower, settling on the collection of broken toys scattered across the floor below.

Her mind drifted from the discomfort, seeking refuge in her memories. She saw her garden as it had been in summer—rows of vegetables growing wild and abundant. Basil plants so full their leaves brushed the ground, releasing their sharp scent whenever the wind stirred them. Squash vines that spiraled through the beds, their broad leaves creating patches of shade where she'd rest during the hottest part of the day. The strawberry patch, hidden beneath protective netting, where berries hung heavy, attracted honeybees.

Mr. Rabbit stood beneath the pear tree at the garden's edge, his shirt dappled with leaf shadows. He reached up, twisting fruit from the lower branches. His laugh carried across the garden when a pear fell before he could catch it, landing with a soft thud in the grass. He always saved the lopsided ones for her, the fruit that grew pressed against a branch or another pear. He'd slide them into the deep pockets of his overalls, patting the bulge with satisfaction.

"The imperfect ones taste sweetest," he'd say, presenting her with his finds at day's end. They'd sit together on the porch steps, juice running down their chins, watching fireflies rise from the grass as darkness fell.

The memory burned with clarity. The way his whiskers twitched when he smiled, first on the left, then the right. The familiar weight of his paw when he'd rest it over hers. She saw him at the door that final morning, every detail etched sharp. His coat buttoned neatly despite the worn spots at the elbows. His mushroom basket swinging at his side.

The ache in her chest rivaled her thirst. She closed her eyes against it, but the images wouldn't fade. They played behind her eyelids in perfect detail.

The door creaked on its hinges.

Her ears shot upward, every muscle tensing. Her heart hammered against her ribs as she pressed herself against the back of the cage, making herself small.

The girl entered in a rush of movement and noise. Her cheeks glowed pink with exertion or excitement. Strands of black hair had escaped from the ribbon meant to hold them back, sticking to her damp forehead. Dirt streaked her yellow dress in long smears, as if she'd been crawling through underbrush or digging in soil.

"You're awake!" Her voice rang too bright in the small space. "I would've come earlier, but Pa let me make the bacon all by myself. I didn't burn it this time. Well, only a little bit on the edges, but Pa said that's how he likes it anyway."

She brought no food or water this time.

The girl crossed the room with quick steps. She climbed onto the chair in front of the cage and sat, her feet swinging beneath the hem of her dress.

She leaned forward until her face was level with the cage.

"You're such a quiet thing," the girl murmured. Her head tilted to one side, studying Mrs. Rabbit with an intensity that made her fur prickle. "That's good, I like that. I knew you were different from the others. They were far too noisy."

Mrs. Rabbit remained perfectly still.

A small hand slipped between the bars, navigating the gaps with ease. The fingers found the space between Mrs. Rabbit's ears. The girl's skin was smooth, surprisingly uncalloused.

The girl petted slowly, methodically, her fingers working through the fur with possessive care.

"You're the prettiest one so far," she said, her voice taking on a dreamy quality. She spoke to herself as much as to Mrs. Rabbit, lost in her own thoughts. "Mama says what I do isn't very nice. She says wild things should stay wild. But how else am I supposed to have dolls to play with? All the old ones are broken now."

Her gaze drifted to the shelf where the porcelain dolls sat in a row.

"Pa says we don't have money for new ones. Says I should be grateful for what I have. But they're no fun anymore. They don't move. They don't have warm fur or little heartbeats." Her fingers found Mrs. Rabbit's pulse, pressing against it gently. "No, I think what I do is very nice. I give them a home. I take care of them. Mama just doesn't understand."

Mrs. Rabbit listened in confusion to the child's ramblings.

She watched the girl's hand withdraw through the bars. The child leaned back in the chair with a satisfied sigh, as if she'd decided something important. Her lips pursed, and she began to hum—that same strange melody from before. When Mr. Rabbit hummed, it brought Mrs. Rabbit great comfort. The girl's humming left her unsettled. The sound filled the shed, bouncing off the walls, nowhere for it to go but back into Mrs. Rabbit's ears.

"Don't worry," the girl said at last. "Tomorrow, we'll get to play. You'll see. Oh! I'll be right back. I forgot to get something."

She jumped out of her chair and ran out the door without another word.

The door swung shut behind her with a bang that shook the walls. But the latch didn't catch properly. The door bounced back, leaving a gap as wide as Mrs. Rabbit's paw. Through that sliver, she could see the forest.

She stared at that gap, that tiny window of escape. Her ears strained forward, catching every sound from beyond the walls. Wind rustled through leaves. Somewhere nearby, another door slammed.

But she heard no other footsteps or voices.

Time crawled forward with agonizing slowness as she waited for the girl to return.

A spider descended from one of the rafters on a thread so fine it was nearly invisible. It stopped midway down, spinning slowly in a draft from the door. Mrs. Rabbit watched it, hypnotized by the rotation. The spider hung there for a few minutes, as if considering its options, before continuing its descent. It reached the floor and scuttled toward a crack between the boards, disappearing into the darkness below.

Mrs. Rabbit's throat felt lined with sand. Her lips had cracked, and she could taste blood when she ran her tongue over them. Even her eyes felt dry, gritty when she blinked.

She tried to distract herself by examining her prison more carefully. The cage was old but sturdy, its wires spotted with rust but nowhere rusted through. The latch mechanism was complex—a sliding bolt held in place by a pin that required thumbs to manipulate. Even if she could reach it, her paws would be useless against it. The base was solid metal, offering no gaps to exploit.

Her survey was interrupted by movement on the shelf. One of the porcelain dolls tilted forward, its weight shifting incrementally. The motion was so slow she almost thought she'd imagined it. Then, without warning, its voice box sputtered to life. Static poured from its closed mouth, a harsh crackling that filled the shed.

Mrs. Rabbit's ears flattened against her skull. The static continued for several seconds before cutting off abruptly.

The doll remained tilted forward, its painted smile unchanged.

She tried standing again, using the cage walls for support. Her good leg took most of her weight while she kept the injured one raised. The position was awkward, uncomfortable, but it was a change from lying down. The cage rattled with her movement.

Standing brought a new perspective but no new hope. Nothing that could help her escape.

She sank back down, exhausted by the small effort. Her strength was fading.

A different sound caught her attention—footsteps outside, but not the quick patter of the girl's bare feet. These steps were light, almost inaudible. They paused near the door.

Through the gap, a shape moved. White fur appeared first, then a pink nose testing the air. A cat slipped through the opening, its body low and cautious. Its fur was long and glossy, catching highlights where the sun touched it. Blue eyes swept the shed's interior, pupils dilated in the dimness.

The cat moved with liquid grace, placing each paw precisely. Its tail twitched at the tip—once, twice. It wove between the scattered tools and crates, investigating scents with delicate sniffs. Its path seemed random but brought it steadily closer to the table.

With a single fluid motion, it jumped onto the chair. A soft trill escaped its throat. It sat for a moment, tail wrapped around its paws, before stepping up onto the table itself.

The cat settled inches from the cage, its blue eyes fixed on Mrs. Rabbit through the bars. Its pupils contracted to vertical slits, then expanded again. It didn't blink.

Mrs. Rabbit didn't move.

The cat leaned forward and sniffed the wire. Its whiskers brushed the metal with tiny pinging sounds. A purr started deep in its throat, a rumbling vibration that seemed too large for its body. The sound was almost pleasant until the cat pushed its nose between the bars, trying to get closer.

One paw followed, sliding through the gap. The cat's toes spread, revealing pale pink pads. Then the claws emerged —curved, sharp, translucent at the tips. They extended slowly towards her.

The cage shifted slightly as the cat pressed harder against it.

It withdrew its paw only to insert it through a different gap, one that brought it closer to Mrs. Rabbit's position. It swiped its extended claws towards her again, but still just out of reach.

The purr took on a frustrated edge. The cat adjusted its position, crouching now, eyes never leaving her.

Another swipe—quick, sharp. The claws caught the fabric of Mrs. Rabbit's dress, snagging the weave. She heard threads pop as the cat pulled back. The purr stopped. A low growl replaced it.

The cat's entire demeanor changed. Its ears flattened. Its fur bristled along its spine. It opened its mouth, revealing fangs, and hissed.

It struck the cage hard with both paws.

Mrs. Rabbit jerked backward. The cage scraped across the table's surface, metal shrieking against wood.

The cat struck again. The cage moved further. Each impact pushed it closer to the table's edge.

She stumbled, trying to keep her balance.

The growl deepened to something primal. The cat reared up on its hind legs and brought both paws down hard. The cage teetered on the table's edge. Tipped. Then fell.

The drop seemed to happen in slow motion. Mrs. Rabbit saw the floor rushing up, had time to brace, but not time to protect her injured foot. The cage hit hard. Her wounded ankle took the impact first, the cage's weight crushing down on it.

A scream tore from her throat, high and terrible.

The cat landed on top of the overturned cage. The wire mesh sagged under its weight, pressing deeper into Mrs. Rabbit's trapped foot. The agony was so intense her vision blurred. She felt consciousness slipping, darkness creeping in from the edges.

But the cat wasn't finished. It crouched on the cage and began reaching through the bars again, more aggressive now that she was pinned. One claw raked across her cheek. She felt the skin part, felt warm blood well up and mat in her fur. Another swipe caught her ribs, tearing through dress and flesh alike.

She pressed herself against the floor, trying to make herself smaller, trying to get away from those reaching claws. But with her foot trapped beneath the cage's edge, she could barely move. The metal frame shook with the cat's efforts. Claws whistled past her ear, caught her shoulder, scraped along her back.

The door burst open with such force it slammed against the wall.

"No!" The girl's voice cracked like a whip. "Bad Kitty! Bad, bad kitty!"

The cat froze, then shrank back. It leaped from the cage and bolted toward the door, letting out a yowl of frustration as it passed the girl.

She stepped aside as it ran past, then slammed the door behind it. "And stay out!" she shouted through the wood.

The girl turned back to the shed's interior. Her face was flushed with anger, but it softened as she approached the overturned cage. She knelt and lifted it with both hands and set it back on the table. The base hit the wood with a solid thud.

"There, you're safe," she said.

Mrs. Rabbit lay crumpled at the bottom of the cage. Blood seeped from the gashes on her cheek and ribs, soaking into her fur and dress. The bandage on her ankle was completely soaked through, red spreading across the white cloth. Drops fell through the wire mesh and pooled on the table's surface.

The girl didn't acknowledge the blood. Her attention had shifted to something she'd brought with her.

Through the haze of pain, Mrs. Rabbit noticed the wooden box in the girl's hands. It had been cobbled together from scrap lumber, each plank a different shade and grain. Some pieces were smooth pine, others rough oak. Bent nails held it all together, hammered in at odd angles. The craftsmanship was crude but functional.

The girl set the box on the table beside the cage. She settled into the chair again cross-legged. Her dress spread around her like a yellow flower. She brushed stray hairs from her face with both hands, tucking them behind her ears, before reaching for the box's latch.

She began to hum again. The strange melody wandered as before, notes climbing and falling without structure.

The lid opened slowly. Inside, lay coils of wire.

They ranged in size from thin as sewing thread to thick as a pencil. Each had been carefully shaped into loops and secured with intricate knots. Some were simple snares. Others showed more complex construction—spring-loaded mechanisms, tension triggers, slip knots designed to tighten under struggle. The metal caught the afternoon light, some lengths dulled with age, others polished bright. A few still carried bits of grass. One had a tuft of gray fur caught in its coils.

They were snares. Dozens of them.

The girl lifted one from its carved groove, a medium-sized snare with a particularly elegant noose. She turned it over in her small hands, fingers tracing the curves and knots with obvious pride. She tested the tension, pulled the noose tight, then loosened it again.

She looked up from the snare to meet Mrs. Rabbit's gaze. Her eyes were bright with excitement.

"Oh, don't worry," she said, laughing. "This one's not for you."

She placed the snare back in the box with reverent care, making sure it lay exactly right. Her fingers lingered on the wire before she closed the lid. The latch clicked shut with finality.

The girl gathered the box into her arms, hugging it against her chest. It looked enormous compared to her small frame, but she held it easily.

"I should go set it up now," she announced. She slid off the chair, the box clutched tight. "I wanted to show you my collection. I'm going to try to get us another friend to play with."

She paused at the door, looking back over her shoulder. "You can never have too many dolls, no matter what Pa says. And the woods are full of them."

Mrs. Rabbit watched her go, unable to move, unable to speak. Blood continued to seep from her wounds, each heartbeat pushing more through the cuts in her flesh.

The girl skipped out of the shed, the box of snares bouncing in her arms. The door swung closed behind her. This time the latch caught properly, sealing with a click.

In the sudden silence, understanding came slowly to Mrs. Rabbit, pushing through the fog of shock and pain.

She hadn't been saved.

She had been caught.

CHAPTER 11

Mrs. Rabbit sat rocking in the cage, gently pressing her thin blanket to the raw places on her skin. Tears streamed down her cheeks as the full weight of her predicament settled over her like a stone.

The little girl had unsettled her from the start—there was a strangeness to her, something Mrs. Rabbit's instincts had recognized but hadn't named. Still, she couldn't quite believe it had been the child who caught her. And after hearing the hounds the other night, there was no longer any doubt: the girl was the daughter of one of the hunters.

Her leg throbbed with renewed agony. Whatever healing the past days had brought unraveled at once, the pain draining what little strength she had left. Escape no longer felt difficult, it felt impossible.

Through her tears, she watched the light outside shift.
The golden hue of late afternoon deepened to amber,
then to burnt orange, as the sun sank toward the horizon.

A breeze picked up outside, rattling the loose
windowpane in its frame.

A final shaft of light cut through the window at a sharp
angle, illuminating the table. Mrs. Rabbit watched the
horizontal beam move across the weathered wood and
doilies, her eyes following its progression with a hollow
kind of attention. The light revealed every scratch and
stain on the table's surface, every ring left by long-ago
cups and bowls.

As the beam slid toward the edge, something caught the
light—a tiny flash from a crack in the table's surface. The
glint lasted only a second before the angle changed and it
disappeared.

Mrs. Rabbit blinked hard. She was certain her mind was
playing tricks. But there it was again. Just inches from her
cage, something buried in the wood gleamed dully.

She pressed against the bars, feeling the cold metal dig

into her chest. The bars were spaced wide enough for her
to push her arm through, though the rough edges bit into
her flesh. She stretched one paw through the narrow gap,
her shoulder socket aching with the strain. Her fingers
extended, claws reaching toward the glinting object. The
tendons in her arm pulled taut, every muscle fiber
straining. Too far. Her claws scraped uselessly against the
table's surface, producing a faint scratching sound, falling
short by mere inches.

Frustration welled in her chest, hot and bitter. She pulled
her arm back, rubbing the sore spot where the bars had
pressed. She studied the distance again, calculating angles
and reach. The object seemed to mock her, winking in
and out of visibility as clouds passed over the setting sun.

She paused, considering her options. The cage was heavy
but not immovable. She had felt it shift slightly as she
pressed against it. *Perhaps...*

Then, with deliberate movements, she began rocking the
cage. She started gently, testing the weight and balance.
Back and forth, gradually increasing force until it shifted
on the table. Metal scraped against wood with each
motion. The harsh scraping seemed to fill the space,

surely loud enough to alert anyone nearby. She froze, ears swiveling, listening for footsteps or voices. Nothing came.

She resumed her efforts. The cage moved incrementally with each rocking motion. Mrs. Rabbit paused frequently to catch her breath, her heart fluttering rapidly beneath her ribs like a trapped bird. Her injured leg protested with each movement, the motion pulled at the skin around her wound. She pushed the sensation aside and continued rocking. Something stirred within her, urging her toward the object.

Another inch gained. The table creaked under the shifting weight. Then another inch. Sweat dampened her fur. The object was almost within reach.

She stretched her paw out again, muscles trembling with exhaustion and strain. Her fingers brushed something small and hard, smooth to the touch. She could feel its circular shape, the slight depression in its center. She hooked one claw around it, the keratin clicking against the hard surface, and drew it closer with painstaking care. It scraped along the wood grain, catching momentarily in a groove before coming free. She pulled it through the bars, nearly dropping it in her eagerness.

When the object finally rested in her palm, time stopped.

A button.

Not just any button—one she recognized instantly.
Round and carved from cherry wood, its grain was visible
even in the dim light. Three small holes in the center
formed a perfect triangle, the edges smoothed to a soft
finish by countless polishings. The wood felt warm in her
palm, as if it still held the memory of life.

One of six she had sewn onto Mr. Rabbit's coat.

She remembered that day clearly. The fire had crackled in
the hearth. Mr. Rabbit sat in his favorite chair, reading
aloud from a book of poetry while she worked. He had
carved the buttons himself, and she had sewn them on
with loving pride, one careful stitch at a time.

Mrs. Rabbit turned the button over with trembling paws.
Etched into the back in tiny, uneven letters were the
initials *Mr. R.*—Mr. Rabbit's mark, the one he placed
on all his belongings.

She could only stare in disbelief.

Mr. Rabbit had been here. In this shed.

Her mind raced through possibilities, each more terrible than the last. Maybe he had been held captive here, just as she was now. She scanned the shed with new eyes, searching for traces of him, some sign he had once been here. Perhaps he had escaped. Or worse, perhaps he was still trapped somewhere nearby.

Her gaze flicked to the small door at the back of the shed, the one the little girl had locked with such determination. It seemed to loom larger now, heavy in the thickening dark.

Evening deepened into twilight. The last of the sunlight vanished, leaving the shed cloaked in shadow. Only a faint glow remained in the western sky, a band of deep violet fading into black.

Mrs. Rabbit clutched the button to her chest. She could feel its edges pressing into her palm, real and undeniable. Renewed courage began to take shape inside her.

She had to escape. Tonight. Not just for herself, but for Mr. Rabbit.

She lifted her head, determination flooding her veins like ice water. The exhaustion remained, the thirst still gnawed, but something stronger had awakened. She would find him. She would bring him home.

But first, she needed out of this cage.

Mrs. Rabbit examined the latch that held the door shut. Her fingers traced its length, feeling every ridge and imperfection in the dark. She couldn't be sure, but it seemed looser than before. Perhaps it had shifted when the cage fell during the cat's attack.

She pushed experimentally against the door. The hinges squeaked softly, but the door didn't budge. Mrs. Rabbit sat back, her mind working through options.

Outside, clouds drifted across the sky, their dark shapes visible through the window. They briefly obscured the rising moon before parting to reveal its silver face. Moonlight spilled through the window, transforming the shed into a world of blue shadows and silver highlights. Every surface seemed to glow.

Night sounds filtered through: an owl's distant call,

hollow and mournful, followed by the low chorus of frogs. Mrs. Rabbit's ears swiveled constantly, tracking each sound, alert for any hint of danger. Somewhere in the little girl's house, a clock chimed.

When the moon reached its zenith, bathing the shed in its brightest light, Mrs. Rabbit knew this could be her only chance to escape.

She turned her attention back to the latch. In the moonlight, she saw a small gap where the metal had bent from the fall. Not much, just a thin space where the latch didn't quite sit flush, but perhaps enough.

She reached through the bars again, ignoring the pain in her arm. Her paw stretched until joints ached and tendons stood out like cords. Her claw barely reached the latch's edge. She could feel the cold metal, slick with condensation from the night air. She pressed against it, trying to push toward the opening. It resisted stubbornly.

She changed angles, contorting her body to attack from below, attempting to lift rather than push. Metal scraped faintly against metal, a thin screech that made her teeth ache, but didn't move enough to clear the loop.

Frustration burned in her chest. So close. She could see exactly what needed to happen—just another centimeter of movement would free the latch.

She worked methodically, pushing and pulling. Rust flakes came away on her fingers, staining fur dull orange and filling her nostrils with the scent of old iron.

The gap widened incrementally. Mrs. Rabbit's breathing quickened with hope and exertion. She glanced toward the window. The moon was still high and bright, but morning would come eventually, and she needed time to search the shed.

Mrs. Rabbit paused, gathering strength. Though her body was exhausted, her resolve remained unshaken.

With one final effort, she pushed against the latch with all remaining strength. Her muscles screamed, her vision grayed at the edges, but she pushed through the pain.

Something shifted. A faint click echoed in the silent shed as the lock slid free from its housing.

The cage door swung open.

CHAPTER 12

Mrs. Rabbit remained frozen for several heartbeats, terrified to move, fearing the door might somehow slam shut again if she dared reach toward it.

Gathering courage, she forced herself forward on trembling legs. The injured ankle screamed in protest as she placed weight on it, but she gritted her teeth and pressed on. Her paws gripped the cage's edge as she carefully stepped through the opening onto the table.

She limped slowly across its cold surface, past scattered doilies and water stains, her claws clicking softly against the polished wood. Every few steps she paused, ears swiveling, listening anxiously for any sign of the girl's approach. The house remained utterly silent. Even the wind had stilled, leaving an oppressive quiet pressing against her ears.

At the table's edge, she saw the girl's chair below. Its seat was lower than the table, offering a manageable descent to the floor. Mrs. Rabbit turned and lowered herself backward, her good leg searching blindly for the chair's surface as her injured leg dragged uselessly. Her claws scraped wood until she found solid footing. The chair wobbled slightly beneath her weight, one uneven leg shorter than the others, but it held firm.

From the chair to the floor required another careful descent. Her muscles, weakened from confinement and injury, shook with effort. The distance seemed greater than it truly was. When her feet finally touched the packed earth, relief surged through her so powerfully that her knees nearly buckled.

Leaning against the table leg for support, she scanned her surroundings. Moonlight illuminated sections of the shed in stark detail, leaving others hidden in impenetrable shadows. The familiar space looked different from this new vantage point. Tools loomed overhead, and shelves stretched toward the ceiling. She needed to search thoroughly, yet quickly.

Mrs. Rabbit began a systematic exploration, limping

along the walls in a slow circuit. Her injured leg forced a halting gait, making progress frustratingly slow. Each step required careful placement of her good foot, then a drag of the wounded limb. The bandage had loosened during her escape from the cage, slipping further with each painful movement.

She swept her paws across the lower shelves, the only ones within her reach. Dust rose in small clouds, tickling her nose. She stifled a sneeze against her shoulder. Glass jars clinked softly as she disturbed them. Most held only the grotesque collections she had already glimpsed from her cage.

She struggled to shift stacked crates with her limited strength, the rough wood leaving splinters embedded in her paws. Behind one stack, she found nothing but cobwebs thick as curtains and the desiccated remains of a small bird. Anxiety mounted as she searched fruitlessly, finding no trace of Mr. Rabbit.

The shed felt larger from this lower perspective, distances stretching unexpectedly. What had appeared as a simple room revealed hidden corners and shadowy alcoves.

She edged past the main door, catching a whiff of night air through a narrow crack at its base—clean and cool, tinged with pine and damp earth. Freedom lay just beyond that barrier, but she couldn't leave yet. Not without knowing Mr. Rabbit's fate.

Finally, she reached the small door at the back of the shed. The brass key dangled just out of reach, tauntingly high. She stretched upward, but her paw fell short by more than a foot.

Mrs. Rabbit scanned the shed urgently for something to stand on. A small wooden crate in the corner proved dangerously unstable when she tested it. Her gaze fell instead on a sturdy, low table pushed against the far wall. It was heavier than it appeared. She gripped its edge and pulled, but it barely budged, its legs sunk deeply into the packed earth from years in place. Bracing her back, she tried again, straining until it loosened with a low, grinding noise.

Dragging the table toward the door was painstakingly difficult. She maneuvered carefully around obstacles, angling it past stacks of clay garden pots. The uneven floor repeatedly snagged the table's legs.

At last, the table stood beneath the key. Mrs. Rabbit climbed onto it, the painted surface slick beneath her paws. It creaked under her weight but held firm. She stretched upward, spine aching, until her claws brushed the cold brass of the key, unable to quite grasp it. Rising precariously onto her toes, she swiped again, wobbling as the table shifted slightly beneath her.

With a final desperate lunge, she knocked the key free. It spun through the air, landing with a clatter on the tabletop. She grabbed it quickly, turning it in her paw, tracing the intricate, age-worn patterns etched onto its surface.

She inserted the key into the paint-crusted lock. It resisted stiffly, metal grinding harshly within. Summoning all her strength, she twisted again. This time, the tumblers reluctantly yielded with a soft click.

The porcelain doorknob, decorated with faded bluebirds, turned surprisingly smoothly beneath her paw. She pulled, but the door stuck stubbornly in its swollen frame. She braced her good leg and tugged harder.

The door gave suddenly, swinging open with unexpected

force and sending her stumbling backward. She crashed into a towering stack of crates, toppling them with a deafening cacophony. Glass shattered, metal tools clanged, and a tin of nails burst open, scattering across the floor.

The noise echoed sharply, each crash setting off another —crates slamming into shelves, shelves rattling violently. Mrs. Rabbit crouched amidst the wreckage, heart pounding furiously, certain the girl would burst through the shed door at any moment.

Through the shed's window, a warm light flickered on in one of the house's upper rooms, spilling softly into the darkness. A shadow shifted behind the glass, a vague shape pressed close to the window.

Mrs. Rabbit held perfectly still, frozen among scattered debris. A broken doll's head lay near her foot, painted eyes staring vacantly upward. At the window, the shadow lingered, shifting slightly, peering outward as if searching. Time stretched interminably. Her muscles cramped, yet she didn't dare move.

Just when she thought she couldn't maintain her pose any

longer, the shadow withdrew. Curtains dropped into place, and the light extinguished, plunging the yard back into darkness.

She waited, counting slowly to one hundred. No further lights appeared. No doors opened. Gradually, she straightened, joints protesting the slow movement.

She turned back toward the open doorway. Beyond the threshold lay absolute blackness, a darkness so complete it appeared almost solid. No moonlight penetrated whatever space awaited beyond; the doorframe was merely a rectangle framing pure void. As she approached, a smell rolled out to meet her, thick and chemical, underscored by a sickly sweetness that turned her stomach.

She couldn't proceed blindly. Her eyes swept the shed until she spotted a candle stub resting on a shelf near the main door. Beside it sat a brass holder and a small box of matches. She retrieved them carefully, moving slowly to avoid further disturbance.

The matchbox was damp, its striking surface worn smooth in places. The first match broke as she struck it, the brittle head crumbling uselessly. The second produced only a weak spark. The third caught at last, flaring with a hiss and the acrid bite of sulfur. She brought the match to the candle's wick, and the flame climbed the string swiftly before settling into a steady, reassuring glow.

Holding the candle before her like a talisman, she approached the open doorway once again. The flame flickered in some unfelt draft, casting dancing shadows along the walls. The darkness beyond swallowed the weak glow, revealing nothing until she reached the threshold. Taking a deep, steadying breath, she stepped across.

The candlelight pressed back the shadows in a tight sphere, illuminating a narrow space smaller than she'd expected. The walls pressed close, papered in faded patterns of tiny yellow roses and pale green leaves. As her eyes adjusted, shapes began to emerge. The flame's glow reflected against glass. Dozens of eyes stared down at her from every direction.

Heads.

Rows upon rows of them, mounted neatly like portraits in a gallery. A young button buck, its slender neck still speckled faintly white. A fox wearing an ornate lace collar, a set of antlers oddly positioned atop its head. A bear sporting a top hat and monocle. Their glassy stares locked onto her, catching tiny flickers of candlelight in lifeless reflections.

A shudder rippled through her. Quickly averting her gaze, Mrs. Rabbit stepped further into the room, emerging from the narrow corridor into what was unmistakably a child's bedroom.

A small bed occupied one wall, draped neatly in a yellow-and-white duvet. Sheer curtains cascaded from the bedposts, and the headboard was elaborately carved with birds and blooming flowers. Opposite stood a dresser painted in white-and-yellow gingham, a large oval mirror rising gracefully above it. On either side of the bed sat small tables, and every available surface—tabletops, shelves, and ledges—was crowded.

A wave of horror churned in Mrs. Rabbit's stomach as she took in the scene. A raccoon dressed in a tiny coat perched stiffly in a wooden boat, a miniature fishing rod clenched rigidly in its paws. Beside it, a mouse family clad in doll clothes crowded a tiny playground; one mouse frozen mid-slide, another paused eternally mid-swing. Nearby, a rat wearing a velvet waistcoat sat upright in a chair, tiny knife and fork glued to its paws, a plate of cheese resting motionlessly on its lap.

Every figure was elaborately costumed: dresses, hats, aprons meticulously crafted. None moved. Squirrels in pastel tutus posed mid-pirouette atop the vanity, tails wired gracefully into frozen ribbons. At the very center of the macabre scene stood a weasel bride dressed in a wedding gown, her veil fashioned from delicate, yellowed lace. Tiny pearl buttons cascaded down her back, each sewn with obsessive care.

Their fur had been brushed meticulously, gleaming in the candlelight. Black threads traced across their pelts like railroad tracks, stitching their bodies together with precise brutality. Glass eyes had been carefully selected—some blue, others green, many a deep, unsettling brown. Every lifeless stare was fixed unblinkingly outward.

Mrs. Rabbit's legs trembled violently. Hot bile rose in her throat, and she pressed one paw against the wall to steady herself. The overwhelming scent of formaldehyde burned sharply at her eyes, mingled with sawdust, cotton batting, and beneath it all, the unmistakable sweetness of decay.

Her candle trembled in her paw, dripping hot wax onto her fur, though she hardly noticed. Her gaze drifted numbly across the room, cataloging every grotesque detail. A shelf crammed full of tiny garments. A sewing basket overflowing with needles and threads in every imaginable color. On a slender table lay rows of glass eyes, neatly sorted by size and hue.

A whisper floated gently through the silence, so faint she nearly missed it.

"Run."

Mrs. Rabbit jerked the candle sharply toward the sound. The flame guttered, shadows leaping wildly across the room. The mounted animals appeared to shift momentarily, but their positions remained fixed, mouths sewn tightly shut.

"Run," whispered another voice, softer and coming from the opposite direction. Her heartbeat stuttered. She spun toward the mice, but their tiny lips were motionless.

More voices rose, a spectral chorus drifting from everywhere and nowhere. Each whisper set her fur bristling with dread.

"Get out."

"Run now."

"She's coming."

The voices overlapped, soft and ghostly, wrapping around her like smoke. She spun in confused circles, desperate to locate their source, but the sound bled from the walls, impossible to pinpoint. Glass eyes glistened in candlelight, reflecting back endless tiny flames.

Perhaps she was losing her sanity. Perhaps her mind had fractured under relentless fear. But real or imagined, the whispers persisted.

"Run."

"Run."

"Run."

Her pulse hammered wildly. As she turned, ready to flee, the candlelight revealed something familiar in the far corner of the room.

A pair of tall rabbit ears stood upright, casting a long shadow across the wall behind them.

Mrs. Rabbit steadied her shaking paw, lifting the candle to look closer.

There, seated stiffly at a small table, was Mr. Rabbit.

CHAPTER 13

A sound of pure shock escaped Mrs. Rabbit's lips, her heart lurching violently inside her chest. The candle nearly slipped from her paw as her vision blurred momentarily, disbelief clouding her senses. Surely, she was hallucinating again, her weary mind conjuring cruel visions of comfort and despair intertwined. Yet this time, Mr. Rabbit sat plainly visible in front of her, solid and real, without that ethereal glow that had marked the image of him days prior.

She stood, paralyzed by the terrible hope that had taken root inside her.

She took a tentative step closer, breath hitching painfully. Every instinct told her not to hope, not to believe, but her heart had already begun to race. Mr. Rabbit sat perfectly still, back turned toward her, his familiar dark coat and proud ears unmistakable. Soft light from the rising sun had started to creep timidly into the room from the open doorway, chasing shadows from their corners and illuminating him in a gray haze. Even from behind, she recognized the slope of his shoulders, the way his ears stood upright and alert.

"Mr. Rabbit?" she breathed softly, almost fearing to disturb the silence. He didn't stir, didn't turn to acknowledge her presence. Her pulse quickened further.

She took another step, then another, the candlelight wavering. On the table before Mr. Rabbit rested a delicate tea set. It was a miniature doll's collection with porcelain cups shaped like crescent moons and a teapot painted with tiny stars. The cups sat empty, though their interiors were faintly stained, as if something dark had once filled them. Beside them, sugar cubes lay untouched upon dainty plates.

Carefully, cautiously, she inched forward again. Each sound, no matter how slight, made her wince with dread, terrified that any wrong movement might break this tenuous spell. Her breath clouded in front of her, faint and fast. Mr. Rabbit did not react. He remained utterly motionless, his posture strangely rigid.

The candle caught his outline more fully now, illuminating the neat hem of his sleeve and the slight wear on his collar.

Her mouth opened again, but no sound emerged. Her thoughts blurred into fragments: *Could he be asleep?* A part of her dared believe he might simply turn and smile at her if she moved just one step closer.

She could no longer contain herself. The last few steps she rushed, desperation overwhelming caution.

"Oh, Mr. Rabbit!" she called, voice louder now, breaking with relief and longing. "I've finally found you!"

But as she reached him, paw outstretched to grasp his shoulder, her heart shattered into sharp fragments. Her paw touched stiff fur and an unnatural hardness beneath. She stumbled backward, nearly dropping the candle, and a sharp gasp escaped her.

Mr. Rabbit stared blankly forward, his beautiful hazel eyes replaced by lifeless glass replicas, glittering in the dim light. His features were frozen, mouth sewn carefully shut with red twine into a forced smile, the stitches meticulous and cruelly precise. His dark coat hung neatly on his rigid frame, though the top button was notably missing.

Mrs. Rabbit's breathing turned shallow, painful sobs wracking her body. She clutched the edge of the table for support as hot tears spilled uncontrollably down her cheeks. The porcelain teacups clinked faintly under her weight, a soft and terrible sound.

"No," she choked out between gasping breaths. "Oh, no—please, no."

Frantic, she leaned forward again, paws grasping at his stiff form, desperately trying to elicit some sign of life. "Wake up, Mr. Rabbit! Please, we have to leave—please, just move!"

But he remained horrifyingly still beneath her paws, silent and immovable. Her heart felt as though it were being torn slowly apart. Her vision blurred further as sorrow mingled violently with panic.

She pressed her forehead to his, breath coming in sharp,

ragged bursts. Her body trembled with a grief too large to contain, rising in waves that left her unmoored.

In her desperation, her paw brushed against something brittle tucked into Mr. Rabbit's coat pocket. Startled, she glanced to find a four-leaf clover, dried yet intact. A sharp ache pierced her heart as she cradled it in her paw. Fresh tears flooded her eyes as grief surged anew, raw and overwhelming.

"I'm so terribly sorry, my beloved," she whispered brokenly, holding the fragile clover close. "I'm so terribly sorry I didn't find you sooner."

The early dawn continued to brighten. Dust floated in the beams like ash. The tea set shimmered faintly.

She closed her eyes for a moment, trying to gather herself, to push back the rising madness. The silence in the room had taken on a texture, thick and weighty, pressing in against her skull. Her ears twitched at every creak. She didn't know how long she stood there, but time bent strangely.

Then, from somewhere distant yet undeniably close, a

muffled voice whispered faintly, breaking the oppressive silence.

"Hello, my four-leaf clover."

Mrs. Rabbit stiffened, every hair standing on end, her heartbeat loud in her ears. The voice belonged unmistakably to Mr. Rabbit, but it echoed oddly, hollow and distant, as if coming from deep inside a cavern. Her gaze flew instinctively to his stitched mouth.

"Mr. Rabbit?" she whispered urgently, leaning closer, desperation coloring her voice.

Minutes passed in aching silence, but no response came.

"Please," she pleaded softly, her voice breaking. "Please say something else."

"It's too late." The voice echoed strangely, seeming to fill the entire room and yet coming from directly in front of her.

"No," Mrs. Rabbit urged fiercely. "It's not too late! We can leave, we can escape from here, together!"

Silence stretched again, heavier this time, oppressive and final.

Confusion and sorrow threatened to overwhelm her completely, tearing through her chest like a wound reopened. Her thoughts raced frantically, searching for impossible explanations. She couldn't tell if she was speaking to a ghost or if her exhaustion and injuries from the past few days had finally stolen her mind.

She fought against the madness she feared was overtaking her. The flame from her candle caught her attention as it bent wildly to one side.

Lost in distress, she did not notice the footsteps behind her. Only the sudden, chilling sound of the door softly clicking shut snapped her violently back to awareness.

Heart leaping to her throat, she spun around sharply.

The little girl stood silently by the closed door, a lantern held aloft. The rising morning sunlight, now blocked by the shut door, left only the lantern's glow illuminating her face, accentuating her calm expression and eyes locked steadily onto Mrs. Rabbit.

Her other arm hung relaxed at her side, hand curled loosely around the brass key Mrs. Rabbit had left in the door.

Mrs. Rabbit watched the girl tuck the key into a side dress pocket.

CHAPTER 14

"You're being a very naughty rabbit," said the little girl, her face blank, voice flat and distant.

She watched Mrs. Rabbit with unblinking eyes, her gaze shifting slowly between the living rabbit and the frozen form of Mr. Rabbit. The silence stretched between them.

Without warning, she turned and walked to the dresser, her bare feet padding softly.

"I see you've found my dolls," she said, pulling open the top drawer with practiced ease. "That's Mr. Clover the Rabbit. He had a four-leaf clover in his pocket, my little lucky charm. I just got him a few days ago. He wasn't very nice. Scratched me too much." She paused, glancing over her shoulder with a small smile. "But he's nice now. Can't scratch anymore."

Mrs. Rabbit's heart hammered against her ribs as she watched the child withdraw a ceramic jug, its surface stained dark with age. Next came a small vial filled with liquid the color of fresh blood, strange symbols etched into the glass that seemed to shift in the light.

"You can't imagine how excited I was to find another bunny!" The girl's voice rose with genuine delight as she approached the tea table. She selected the empty cup opposite Mr. Rabbit, the porcelain moon catching the light. "Mr. Clover needs a wife, and I plan on throwing you two a wonderful wedding once I make you one of my dolls."

Mrs. Rabbit remained frozen, every muscle locked in terror as the child returned to the dresser. The girl's movements were precise, ritualistic, as she poured the dark liquid into the teacup. Three drops fell from the vial, each one spreading through the tea like blood through water. She stirred the mixture with her index finger, humming that wandering melody.

"I have the prettiest dress for you too," she continued, settling cross-legged on the floor across from Mr. Rabbit. The teacup clinked softly as she placed it before

Mrs. Rabbit. "I made it all by myself from one of my old doll's dresses. Don't worry though, I made it brand new. Not a hand-me-down at all."

Mrs. Rabbit found herself trapped between her husband's still form and the child, her injured leg trembling with the effort of standing. The girl reached for a sugar cube, dropping it into the strange tea where it bobbed on the surface, slowly staining red.

"Mr. Clover is going to be so happy to have a wife! And such a pretty one, too. Right, Mr. Clover?" She giggled, clapping her hands once with childish glee. "And I think I'll call you Mrs. Hellebore. Isn't that so cute? It's Mama's favorite flower, the one she grows in the back garden. Mr. Clover and Mrs. Hellebore—oh, that's just perfect!"

The words washed over Mrs. Rabbit in waves of horror. These weren't dolls at all, but creatures like herself, trapped forever in this child's twisted playroom. Her mind raced, searching desperately for escape routes, for any possibility of freedom. But her injured ankle throbbed with each heartbeat, and she knew she could never outrun the girl, not in this state.

"You've been a pretty naughty rabbit these past few days," the girl said, tilting her head like a curious bird. "But maybe you're just ready to play. I thought you needed longer to heal, but I think you're ready now. Mr. Clover has seemed lonely, so he'll be happy to finally have you join our tea parties."

Mrs. Rabbit's gaze darted to Mr. Rabbit, trying not to betray their connection. *Could she leave him here? Return with help—Mr. Fox, despite his injuries, or fierce Mr. Badger?* But even as the thought formed, she knew it was impossible. She couldn't abandon him here.

"I'm hoping I can catch a little baby rabbit next," the girl continued dreamily, "so we can be one big happy family. Wouldn't that be so lovely?"

Mrs. Rabbit drew in a shuddering breath through her nose, having forgotten to breathe as the full weight of understanding crashed over her. Every mounted head, every costumed figure, had once been alive, had once been trapped or hunted. Now they were all kept here, little dolls forced into dresses, made to play pretend.

Depression settled over her like a wet blanket, making her

limbs feel impossibly heavy. The key was tucked safely in the girl's pocket. The door was locked. Her ankle barely supported her weight. Even if by some miracle she managed to escape this room, she'd never make it through the woods.

And she couldn't leave Mr. Rabbit. Not like this.

"Drink your tea," the girl said, breaking the silence. "I promise it tastes good."

Mrs. Rabbit stared at the crescent moon cup. The sugar cube floated on the surface. A cloying sweetness rose from the liquid, making her stomach turn. Every instinct screamed it was poison.

"Come on," the girl urged, pushing the cup closer with one finger. "Drink."

Around them, the glass eyes of countless victims watched in witness. Mrs. Rabbit felt their gaze like physical weight, pressing down on her shoulders. She glanced at her ankle where fresh blood seeped through the bandage, her good leg beginning to go numb from bearing all her weight.

"I promise it won't hurt," the girl said, her smile never wavering. "And we'll get to be a big happy family! Just imagine—you and Mr. Clover, happily married, with a little baby rabbit, and we get to play tea parties every day!"

"Come on, drink," the girl repeated, impatience creeping into her voice. She lifted the cup and leaned across the small table, pressing it toward Mrs. Rabbit's mouth.

Without thought, purely on instinct, Mrs. Rabbit's paws shot out and grabbed the cup. In one swift motion, she flung the contents into the child's face.

The girl shrieked, a sound of pure rage that pierced the morning air. "Pa! PA!" she screamed, rubbing frantically at her eyes as the liquid burned her eyes.

Adrenaline surged through Mrs. Rabbit's veins, lending her strength she didn't know she possessed. Mr. Rabbit wouldn't want her to give up. She had to escape, had to survive, and then she would return for him.

She dropped to all fours and lunged for the girl's pocket, her paw closing around the brass key just as the child began to rise. The tea set crashed to the floor, porcelain shattering into a thousand pieces as the table overturned.

Mrs. Rabbit ran, the mounted heads calling after her as she passed through the narrow corridor.

"Run."

"Run."

"Run."

Their voices merged into a chant that followed her to the door. She reached up, but the lock remained frustratingly out of reach. A stack of children's books sat near the entrance, fairy tales with bright covers. She dragged them beneath the lock, climbed with shaking legs, and inserted the key.

The lock clicked open. But before she could pull the door wide, it swung inward with tremendous force. Mrs. Rabbit clung to the key, her body suspended as the door pressed her against the wall.

"Ethel? What's going on?" A man's voice boomed through the space, deep and commanding.

The girl ran to him, still wiping at her face, tears streaming down her cheeks. He bent low, using the hem of his flannel shirt to clean away the liquid. "What happened, little one?"

"My bunny! She's a bad, bad bunny!"

"Hush now," Pa said, his voice gentle but firm. "You'll be alright. I thought I warned you to be careful. You know what happened last time."

He tousled her hair affectionately, then glanced around the room. His bulk filled the small space—he had to duck beneath the low ceiling, his broad shoulders nearly touching both walls of the corridor. His gaze swept past the mounted heads, the scattered tea set, before landing on the door.

There, still hanging from the key, was Mrs. Rabbit.

He plucked her from her perch with two fingers pinching the scruff of her neck, lifting her to eye level. His face was weathered and tan, with deep lines around his eyes. She smelled tobacco from his breath. "Well, that's new. Never seen a black rabbit from the wild before." He turned her slowly, examining her like a curiosity. "Now Ethel, I've told you to be careful with your animals. They may have diseases."

"She is not an animal!" Ethel stamped her foot. "She is my doll!"

"As you say," he chuckled, the sound rumbling from deep in his chest. He placed Mrs. Rabbit into his daughter's waiting arms. "Clean up before your Mama sees you at breakfast. You know how she gets."

The door closed with a decisive thud.

Ethel's arms constricted around Mrs. Rabbit like iron bands, squeezing until her ribs creaked. Mrs. Rabbit struggled, claws raking desperate furrows in the girl's skin, but Ethel only held tighter, crushing the air from her lungs. Black spots danced at the edges of her vision as her struggles weakened, then ceased.

The girl carried her to the dresser and laid her on her back atop it. One small hand pressed firmly down against Mrs. Rabbit's chest while the other retrieved the vial of blood-red liquid.

"It's time," Ethel whispered.

Mrs. Rabbit tried to clamp her mouth shut, but the girl used the vial's edge to pry her jaws apart. The liquid poured down her throat, burning like fire, tasting of bitter flowers and sharp chemicals. She coughed and sputtered, but Ethel's hand remained steady until the last drop had been administered.

"There." The girl carefully returned the vial to its drawer. "That wasn't so bad. But you are a naughty rabbit. I thought you were nice, but you hurt me. See?"

She held up her arm where three parallel scratches wept blood, the skin already beginning to bruise.

"It's okay though," Ethel continued, her voice returning to its cheerful lilt. "You'll get to be my doll now, and we're going to have so much fun. Just wait, you'll see."

Mrs. Rabbit tried to focus on the child's words, but they seemed to come from very far away. A creeping numbness began in her toes, spreading upward through her legs like ice water in her veins. Her arms grew heavy, then her head, until she couldn't move at all.

The world narrowed to a pinpoint of light.

Then darkness claimed her, and the girl's voice faded to nothing.

CHAPTER 15

A metallic melody drifted through the darkness, slow and uneven. Mrs. Rabbit recognized it before she fully woke. It was the strange tune the little girl often hummed, now playing from a music box. The mechanism caught and stuttered, making the familiar melody stagger and lurch, as if the box itself were broken or very old.

The light came next, but it was wrong. It fractured and bent in ways that light should not, splitting into prismatic shards that hurt to perceive. The world assembled itself slowly—first shadows, then shapes, then colors bleeding together. Everything bore a purple tinge, as though she viewed the world through stained glass.

When her vision finally settled, Mr. Rabbit stood before her.

He had been dressed in fresh clothes, a long coat of deep forest green over a cream linen shirt with small buttons done up to his throat. Dark brown trousers completed the ensemble. His fur gleamed with recent brushing, each strand lying perfectly in place. In his paw, something glinted gold. A ring.

They were no longer at the tea table. Soft fabric pressed beneath her, the girl's bed, she realized, though they stood atop a piece of weathered wood that served as a makeshift platform. The yellow-and-white duvet spread around them like a meadow of fabric flowers.

A figure in the dresser mirror caught her attention. A rabbit in lavender stood reflected there, herself, though recognition came slowly. She wore a gown of pale purple silk, delicate lace adorning the sleeves and high collar. A row of tiny pearl buttons ran down the front. A thin veil of matching lavender obscured her face. The lantern on the dresser cast reflections in the mirror, creating strange distortions within the room.

In her own paw was another gold ring.

Mrs. Rabbit willed her legs to move. Nothing happened.

She tried her arms next, straining with every fiber of her being to lift them, to drop the ring. Her body remained terribly still.

She tried to open her mouth to call Mr. Rabbit's name, but her jaw would not obey. She assumed the child's poison had left her paralyzed, and hoped the effects would soon wear off so she could still attempt to escape.

The door burst open, flooding the room with afternoon sunshine so bright it was blinding. Mrs. Rabbit's vision went white completely before gradually returning, the purple haze now threaded with golden afterimages.

The little girl entered wearing clothes far too large for her small frame. A black suit jacket hung past her knees, its sleeves rolled up multiple times to free her hands. Black trousers pooled around her feet. Her dark hair had been arranged in pigtails, each secured with a white satin bow. She clutched a small book bound in cracked leather.

She positioned herself before them with great ceremony, clearing her throat importantly.

"Dearly beloved," she began, then giggled at her own

seriousness. "We are gathered here today to join these two rabbits in matrimony."

She paused, flipping through the book's pages with one finger, squinting at the text.

"Mr. Clover," she announced, "do you take Miss. Hellebore to be your wife?"

The girl pitched her voice low and gruff: "I do."

Another giggle escaped her, high and delighted.

"And Miss. Hellebore, do you take Mr. Clover to be your husband?"

This time her voice rose to a squeaky falsetto: "I do!"

"Then by the power vested in me," she proclaimed, spreading her arms wide so the suit jacket billowed like wings, "I now pronounce you husband and wife! You may kiss the bride."

She burst into applause, clapping so hard the book tumbled from her grasp. Still grinning, she reached for

Mrs. Rabbit's veil, lifting it carefully over her head. The fabric caught momentarily on her ears before settling behind her.

Even with the purple veil removed, the world remained strangely tinted. The girl manipulated Mrs. Rabbit like a doll, tilting her forward until her lips pressed against Mr. Rabbit's in a mockery of a kiss. The contact was brief before the child positioned her upright again.

"Perfect!" The girl squealed, resuming her enthusiastic applause. "Oh, what a beautiful wedding! Now we all get to be together forever and ever and ever!"

As the little girl celebrated, Mrs. Rabbit had caught sight of herself in the mirror. With her veil removed, she saw her face with clarity. Where her eyes should have been, brown glass spheres stared back, flat and lifeless. Her mouth had been sewn shut with careful stitches of lavender thread, pulled tight to create a gentle smile.

The panic she'd felt before was nothing compared to the horror that crashed over her now. She stared at her reflection, unable to look away, unable to close her eyes.

A single tear rolled down Mrs. Rabbit's cheek, tracing a wet path through her dark fur.

"That's never happened before," the girl said softly. She stopped clapping, her smile fading into a puzzled expression.

Midnight Fables is a collection of standalone
gothic fairytales—literary, atmospheric, and
quietly unsettling. Inspired by the idea of creating
the next generation's Goosebumps for older
readers, the series blends the nostalgia of Peter
Rabbit with the eerie wonder of Coraline, and the
emotional depth of Watership Down.

SHOP MORE TITLES

WWW.MIDNIGHTFABLES.COM